STEELE'S WAR:
THE WOMAN

George G. Gilman

NEW ENGLISH LIBRARY/TIMES MIRROR

For:
Gabrielle
because I promised – not
what I threatened

A New English Library Original Publication, 1980

© 1980 by George G. Gilman

First NEL Paperback Edition July 1980

NEL Books are published by
New English Library Limited from
Barnard's Inn, Holborn,
London EC1N 2JR.
Made and printed in Great Britain by
Hunt Barnard Printing Ltd.,
Aylesbury, Bucks.

45004630 3

AUTHOR'S NOTE

LONG-time readers of the Western series featuring Edge will recall that I wrote a sequence of books devoted largely to his experiences during the War Between the States. From mail I have received it is obvious that many readers greatly enjoyed these books: not least because of the way in which they showed how Edge developed from a raw Iowa farm boy into the killer-without-compunction he was seen to be in the first book of the series.

Much of this mail asked why I did not write a similar sequence of books about Adam Steele's baptism of fire during the Civil War.

So, believing that the customers should be given what they want, this and the next three books in the series will cover the Civil War period from the viewpoint of Adam Steele.

In the Edge war books I used a technique of alternating between a running contemporary story and flashbacks to the past. In this and the succeeding three books of the Steele series, I have modified this method – sandwiching an entire episode from the war years between two halves of a short story.

Each book will therefore contain two stories – one contemporary and one from the past of the Virginian. Each of them complete in themselves. But, as always in both Edge and Steele books, they will be written as much like a serial as a series and the enjoyment of readers will undoubtedly be enhanced if the books are read in numerical – that is to say, chronological – order.

This assumes that they will be enjoyed at all. I hope they will be. Particularly by those readers who have written to ask, in essence: 'What did Adam Steele do in the war, Mr Gilman?'

THE WOMAN: Part One

THE skinny old man who tended the Gold Gulch way station peered through the billowing cloud of grey dust, licking his thin lips in eager anticipation.

The dust had been raised by the skidding arrival and frantic departure of the Friday westbound stage. Running two hours behind schedule. The driver had held the team in check for just a few seconds. Time enough for the man riding shotgun to toss down a valise from the roof of the Concord. And for a brief exchange of words between the driver up on the seat and the old-timer in the way station doorway.

'Nothin' and nobody to pick up, Bill? Just like always?'

'Like always, Charlie!'

'One gettin' off for a change! Broke a damn wheel spoke and we're runnin' late. Gotta make up time or Jack and me'll lose our bonuses! See you next Tuesday!'

Charlie cracked the reins and had the rig rolling again before he finished explaining the reason for the rush. So that turning wheel-rims and pumping hooves erupted more dust from the little-used trail: to make denser the temporary veil which hung between the old-timer on the way station threshold and the passenger who had disembarked through the far door of the stage.

Any passenger who got off the stage at Gold Gulch would have been of interest to old Bill Turner – simply as a fellow human being. For they were scarce in this section of the San Simon Valley and although old Bill enjoyed being alone, it was good to talk to somebody from time to time.

But he was particularly intrigued by this passenger because, just for a second or so while the stage was halted, he was sure that it was the skirt of a gown he had glimpsed through the whirling dust beneath the Concord. And in the ten years he had been running the way station, no woman had ever got off the stage here – unless to do what she had to do in the facilities at the rear and get right back on board again.

'My goodness me, sir. I do not believe I have ever in my life had such a terrifying journey.'

The woman saw Bill Turner before the old-timer was able to distinguish her through the settling dust. Which was understandable, he realised, as he stepped out of the way station doorway and received a clear impression of her. For she was less than half his near seventy years of age so that her faculties were bound to be sharper.

Just turned thirty, he guessed as the last dust motes settled and the mid-morning Arizona sun glared unimpeded upon the barren expanse of the San Simon Valley surrounding the way station. A petite redhead who stood about five-three tall and weighed in the region of a hundred pounds. With a build that, although slim, was in no way boyish – from the way the high-necked bodice of her gown contoured the woman's torso.

The white dress, cut on plain and simple lines, was creased, dust-smeared and sweat-stained from the stage ride. And several strands of her long, copper-coloured hair had worked loose and hung lankly from her chignon. The make-up which had probably been carefully applied to her handsome face was smudged and discoloured by dust.

But despite her dishevelled appearance, she was obviously an attractive woman who under the best of circumstances would be beautiful. And, as he raised a hand to touch the front of his bald head, at the same time stooping to pick up her valise, Bill Turner was certain his opinion owed little to the fact women were few and far between in this piece of territory. Long past his prime and starved of female company he may have been, but he could still pick out the wheat from the chaff in the matter of handsome women.

'Charlie and Jack are still young enough to have ambitions, ma'am,' he said, glancing out along the west trail to where the stage was hidden by an elongated dust cloud, the sound of its hell-for-leather progress diminishing fast. 'And ambitions are somethin' that need cash money to get. Bonuses for runnin' the stage to time is in cash money. You want to come on inside the station and sit on somethin' that ain't movin'?'

The woman was using the backs of both hands to brush

dust from her gown. Then she reached to the nape of her neck and felt the loose strands of hair. And grimaced as she groaned: 'Goodness, I must look a sight.'

The dungaree-dressed old-timer lit his thin face with a smile that showed just a few discoloured teeth in the lower gum. 'If you'll take no offence, ma'am, I'd like to say a sight for sore eyes. But I know how womenfolk feel about wantin' to look their very best all the time. There's a place out back of here. With water and soap and a towel. Mirror, too.'

He gestured with his free hand towards the way station doorway and the shade beyond.

'I certainly would appreciate the opportunity to freshen myself up some, sir,' she said as she abandoned her attempt to repair the damage to the chignon. And was suddenly anxious as she tried to peer with her pale green eyes into the interior of the frame-built, single-storey station that was little more than a flat-roofed shack.

Both her expression and a slight tremor in her Deep-South-accented voice revealed her sudden nervousness. 'I presume, sir, there is nobody else inside?'

'No, ma'am, there ain't.'

Her sigh of relief was visible but not audible. And she followed this with a bright smile. 'It's Miss. Miss Lucy Girard. Perhaps Mr Lorrimer has spoken to you of me?'

Now it was Bill Turner who expressed concern. Which she did not see deepen the lines of the old-timer's face for she had swept past him with a rustle of petticoats to go into the way station.

'I was wonderin' why you got off the stage at Gold Gulch, Miss Girard,' he said pensively as he followed her inside. 'Hardly anyone ever does, except them bent on prospectin' the Dos Cabezas Mountains. And most times them fellers come in on horseback or ridin' a mule.'

'Through here?' Lucy asked, pointing to a closed door.

'Right,' Turner confirmed, setting down her valise on one of the several wooden seats that lined two walls of the way station's public area. 'Ain't much, but there's fresh soap and the water and towel is clean. Keep everythin' around here clean as a man of my age can. On account it's the only thing I got to fill the time.'

She would not have heard most of what he said since she had gone through the doorway at the rear of the room. The old-timer shrugged and pushed open a closed door in a side wall — to go through into his one-room living quarters. There he lifted a blackened pot off the top of a pot-bellied stove and poured himself a tin cup of coffee, which he took out to the front of the way station, dragging across the threshold the most conveniently placed chair. Here he sat down, sipping the coffee and gazing out across the cactus, mesquite, brush and rock featured valley floor towards the ridges of the Dos Cabezas range far to the south-west. Seeing most of what he looked at as a blur. Frowning as, in the silence of the desert country, he listened to the small sounds made by Lucy Girard out back.

Then, as he drained the cup of its contents, he muttered: 'Well, I'll be. Dan Lorrimer and a woman.'

He had not realised his thought had been spoken aloud until Lucy said: 'You know Mr Lorrimer, sir?'

He stood up and turned to look across the spartan public room as her tread sounded on the floor boarding. 'He kin of yours, miss?'

It took a few moments for his old eyes to adjust from the harshness of the Arizona sunlight to the shade of the way station's interior.

'He will be very soon. Mr Lorrimer and I plan to be married.'

With the innate skill developed by experience of her gender, the woman had used whatever was in her small purse and the mere basics of cleanliness provided out back to transform her previous travel-stained appearance. There was little she had been able to do about her gown, but her face and hair had received sufficient attention to make the very best of what she had been endowed with by nature. Which in the view of Bill Turner made her response to his query even more incredulous. He felt his frown deepen – become something close to a scowl maybe – and was on the point of voicing his feelings. But he held back the words. Instead, asked:

'You want a cup of coffee? Always have a full pot on the stove when a stage is due.'

'I surely would appreciate that, sir.'

He nodded and shuffled across the room and into his private quarters. As Lucy, showing no sign that she had seen his frown or heard anything amiss in his tone, stepped outside to sit on the chair. Where, for several moments, she breathed deeply of the clean, hot air and allowed her eyes to scan the almost barren landscape which the old man had recently surveyed.

But suddenly her attitude changed. Her posture altered from one of relaxed enjoyment to rigid tension. As she caught her breath and her smile was replaced by a frown of anxiety. And her eyes stared fixedly at a single point out across the valley's desert floor.

A moving point. Closing with the isolated way station.

'Here you are, miss. Hot and strong. Just what a person needs after a long stint of hard travellin'.'

The woman took the steaming tin cup absently – automatically – from Bill Turner as he halted beside the chair. Then asked: 'Could this be Mr Lorrimer coming now, sir?'

Turner looked from the anxious face out in the direction she was peering. 'You see a man out there? Comin' outta the hills?'

'Yes, don't you?'

'Not yet, miss. These old eyes of mine don't see too well lately. But if a man's ridin' outta the hills, could well be Dan Lorrimer. Or any one of a couple of dozen prospectors that work claims all over the Dos Cabezas. He know you were due to arrive at Gold Gulch today?'

The possibility that the man out in the desert might be somebody other than Lorrimer acted to release some of Lucy's tension. And she was able to drink the coffee and divide her attention between the lone rider and the old man standing beside her.

'No. No, he doesn't know. He just knows I wrote him that I'd get here as soon as I could. And he wrote back that he or his friends were by the station frequently. And that you – you're Mr Turner?'

'That I am.'

'That you would take care of me until somebody came by to give me a ride out to his claim. Did he not mention the arrangement to you? When he brought the letter here?'

The old-timer shook his head as his squinting eyes caught a first sight of the lone rider who had closed to within two miles of the station. 'No, miss. I must've handled the letter and no mistake. But I can't recall that Dan Lorrimer give it to me. Ain't nothin' strange about that, though. Him and his buddies, they kinda take turns to come here. Send stuff out or pick up supplies. Reckon the feller that brung the letter plain forgot to give me the message. Ain't many of the fellers out in the hills very bright.'

Lucy vented a deep sigh, as if in response to the effort of

11

quelling her anxiety. Then rose to her feet and spread a wan smile across her face as she reached into the station to pick up the valise.

'Well, it would seem I have no need to trouble you further, Mr Turner. Somebody is coming for me right now.'

Perhaps a full minute passed in silence between the old man and the woman as they stood at the way station doorway, looking out towards the approaching rider who held his horse to an easy walk. Then Turner said:

'Ain't no one I ever seen before, miss.'

He was aware that her tension eased even more as a result of his reply. And she, as she turned to look at him, saw the extent of his curiosity on his time-lined features.

'My, you must think me very odd, sir. Here am I, a woman soon to be a bride, acting the very opposite of happy at the prospect of being with my future husband.'

Turner shuffled his feet and looked away from her wide, bright, pale green eyes smiling at him – embarrassed that she had seen his expression. 'Don't matter what I thinks, miss,' he growled. 'I've near had my life and I'm real lucky the stage line company still finds a use for me. Tendin' the needs of folk that usually only stop over for a couple of minutes. The lives of those folks ain't no business of mine.'

'Nonsense,' she chided, setting down the hardly touched cup of coffee on the chair. 'There's no harm in conversation as a pleasant way to pass the time. And I am certainly not ashamed to tell you that I and Mr Lorrimer have never met. I do not intend to keep it a secret that I am what is known as a mail-order bride.'

As she spoke, she saw Turner's expression alter from embarrassment, to interest, to concern. And as she witnessed this, she was also attacked by anxiety again. This as the stranger rode close enough for the clop of his mount's hooves to be heard. Then the woman tore her gaze away from the suddenly pitying eyes of the old-timer to stare at the rider and call: 'My name is Lucy Girard, sir! Have you come to fetch me?'

The stranger reined his horse to a halt on the far side of the trail and raised a gloved hand to touch the broad brim of his Stetson. And grinned as he answered:

'You're the most fetching thing I've seen in a long time, ma'am. But I reckon it's not my lucky day. You're expecting somebody else. I'm Adam Steele.'

12

He swung wearily down from the saddle and led his black gelding across the final few yards to the front of the way station. A short man, standing not much more than five feet six inches, built on lean lines which, from the manner he moved, suggested his frame commanded a compact strength. He had a halfway handsome face, tanned and lined by many years of exposure to the elements. A long face with regular features: the eyes coal-black and the mouthline gentle. There were still a few reddish hairs in the otherwise grey sideburns that he wore long but neatly trimmed. Despite the half-day's bristles on his firm jaw and lean cheeks, the smile made him appear almost boyish. But when the expression was replaced by impassiveness, it was possible to place his age in the late thirties.

His style of dress made him seem at odds with the harsh south-western landscape that surrounded him. A grey suit cut on city lines, a lace-trimmed white shirt, a red vest and black Stetson and boots which – although dust clung to them – still retained a look of store-bought newness. Not so the grey, silken kerchief which hung loosely around his neck and the skin-tight black buckskin gloves on his hands: for these showed many signs of long, hard wear.

He did not wear a gunbelt and the only visible weapon was a rifle which jutted from a boot slung from the right front of his saddle. A saddle, with its accoutrements, which also looked newly purchased.

'Bill Turner, sir,' the old-timer greeted brightly, liking the looks of the newcomer. Welcoming the opportunity he provided to evade the issue which Lucy Girard had obviously intended to raise. 'I run the stage line way station here at Gold Gulch. But that don't mean I only serve stage line passengers. Can be of any help to you, happy to oblige.'

The woman had set down her valise, picked up the cup from the seat and lowered herself on to the chair.

'Your coffee smells good and the horse would be grateful for watering, feller,' Steele answered, his Virginian roots clear to hear in his voice.

'Take care of both those needs right away, sir,' Turner said and reached for the reins of the gelding.

Steele surrendered the animal to the old-timer, but slid the rifle from the boot as the horse was led around to the rear of the way station. It was a Colt Hartford revolving model, with a gold plate screwed to the side of the fire-scorched rosewood stock: the precious metal glinting in the sunlight as he canted the rifle to his left shoulder.

'Did I interrupt something, ma'am?' he asked as he moved on to the threshold of the Way station, into the shade.

For long moments, Lucy Girard appeared not to have heard the question. As she continued to sit rigidly on the chair, the cup of cooling coffee clutched in both hands on her lap and eyes staring fixedly out across the desert. Then she glanced over her shoulder at the dudishly attired Virginian and shrugged her slender shoulders.

'It is of no consequence. I have known from the outset the risks involved. Perhaps it is better that I discover my fate at first hand. Rather than to go to meet it with my mind filled by rumours of what it will be.'

Steele looked down wryly on to her recently repaired chignon. 'Your business is your own, ma'am,' he said. 'And if you intended to make it mine by – '

'I'm sorry,' she cut in. 'I had no intention of sounding mysterious in an attempt to arouse your interest. And neither do I have any reason to be rude to you. But I would appreciate it if you would mind your own business. Here, from what I drank of it, the man makes fine coffee.'

She hurled the tepid remains of her coffee across the trail and then handed the cup over her shoulder towards Steele. As he took it, she glanced back at him and despite an effort to conceal her true feelings with manufactured loftiness, the Virginian saw plainly the worry in her pale green eyes. Which expanded and found vocal outlet in a gasp before she swung her head away from him when he said:

'Maybe one of those fellers is coming to get you, ma'am.'

There were three of them. Riding fast ahead of a dust cloud on a route parallel and some two miles to the west of the line Steele had taken out of the Dos Cabezas Mountains: then veering to the side to close with the way station over the shortest distance.

'There you go, sir,' Bill Turner said, taking the empty cup from Steele's hand and replacing it with a full one. 'Horse is taken care of. Fifty cents is all it'll cost you.'

The Virginian rested his rifle against the doorframe while he dug for coins in his pants pocket. Then lost the attention of the old-timer as Turner saw the renewed tension in Lucy's attitude and strained to see the reason for it.

14

'Somebody else comin'?' he asked quickly.

'Three,' Steele answered as the money was accepted absently. 'Riding horses that'll need water worse than mine.'

The old-timer shot a pitying glance down at the seated woman. 'Three, uh? Reckon it'll be Dan Lorrimer and his buddies. Rocky Parker and Jay Flynt. Only three gold grubbers in the hills I ever known to run together like real buddies. Rest of them out there are loners with no time for each other. But them three are closer than brothers.' He had shifted his weak eyes to the impassive face of the coffee-drinking Steele. But looked down again at Lucy Girard as he concluded: 'Share and share alike. Everythin' they got and everythin' they get.'

From the words the old man spoke and his tone of voice, and the way in which the woman shuddered once and then became like a granite-carved statue on the chair, Steele decided he knew the basics if not the details of the kind of situation he had rode into. Then, with an expression of pleading on his thin face, Bill Turner supplied the keystone: 'Dan Lorrimer and Miss Girard ain't never met. But a weddin's planned.'

'Oh, my dear God!' the woman gasped.

'Reckon preachers are thin on the ground in this part of the country,' Steele drawled. 'Gives you plenty of time to change your mind and you won't be the first woman to say no after saying yes.'

'No ain't a word Dan Lorrimer takes to, sir,' Turner growled as the trio of riders came close enough to the way station for him to see them. 'And that sure is him and his buddies.'

'Please!' Lucy rasped, suddenly forcing herself up from the chair and backing towards the doorway. So that Steele had to snatch his rifle away from the frame before she kicked it over. 'I never expected anything like this. I came out here in good faith. The letters sounded so genuine. Please help me!'

She had managed to wrench her gaze away from the three riders. Looked first at the impassive-faced Steele, groaned and swung her head to direct a tacit plea to the old-timer who had backed into the way station. But Turner's face promised nothing more tangible than pity. Mixed in with much the same brand of fear as she felt.

Lorrimer, Parker and Flynt were slowing their horses now. And above the less frenetic beat of hooves, one of them could be heard: shouting in tones of high excitement.

15

'Hey, Bill Turner! We struck it rich, you old bastard! Get that case of liquor out! We're celebratin'!'

There was a shuffling of feet beside Steele as Lucy backed all the way into the station. And her place on the threshold was taken by the old-timer.

'Happens once in awhile, sir,' Turner muttered, running the back of a hand across his lips. 'Somebody out there in the hills finds a big nugget and he comes in here actin' like it's another Sutter Creek strike. And get drunk on the liquor I keep here. On account of there's a kinda unwritten law that the only liquor at the claims is for medical reasons.'

The men had ridden close enough now to be seen in detail, against the backdrop of desert and ridges no longer clouded by dust. Heavily bearded and filthy dirty men who had not washed up in a very long time. Dressed in ragged shirts and pants, scarred work boots and battered hats. Riding ill-cared-for geldings. All aged in their mid-forties.

'How goes it, stranger!' the one who had done the shouting greeted as he and the men flanking him reached the trail, reined in their mounts and swung down from their simple saddles. 'Join the celebratin' and welcome. You picked a fine day to reach Gold Gulch. And I ain't meanin' about the weather, no sir.'

He was grinning broadly, showing tobacco-stained teeth. Taller by a head than his two companions, he was less broadly built than them. A lot uglier, with thick lips, a prominent nose and small eyes.

'Good to know you found a big one, Dan,' Turner said with forced enthusiasm. 'You fellers deserve a break. Jay. Rocky.'

He nodded to Flynt and Parker. The former with a square build and features who eyed Steele with unconcealed suspicion: the latter a fat man with a hanging belly and breasts that were almost womanly who had a fixed foolish grin on his fleshy face.

The Virginian finished his coffee and made one nod serve as a greeting for all three men as the reins of the horses were handed to Parker.

'This here's Mr Adam Steele,' Turner introduced while the fat man hitched all the horses to a single iron hook at a corner of the Way station. 'Stopped by just for coffee and to rest up his horse.'

'Didn't look like no prospector to me,' Jay Flynt growled.

16

'What about that liquor, Bill?' Lorrimer insisted, licking his thick lips still drawn apart in the grin. 'And some shade from your roof, you old bastard. Got what it takes to pay for our needs.'

He delved into a pocket of his pants and then opened his fist, extending his hand towards the two men in the doorway. To show on his work-gnarled, dirt-ingrained palm an irregular-shaped nugget of perhaps ten ounces in weight.

'Near pure as I've ever seen,' Rocky Parker said in an awed tone as he rejoined the group at the way station doorway.

'Hell, I didn't have to see it, Dan,' Turner said quickly. 'Your credit's always been good with me, you know that.' He shot a glance back over his shoulder and saw that the public room of the station was empty. 'Come right on in, boys. And I'll get the liquor.'

'You ain't a talker, are you, mister?' the sour-faced Flynt growled as he brushed by Steele, the last of the three prospectors to follow Turner across the threshold.

'What do you want to hear from me, feller?' the Virginian asked.

'The reason you tote that rifle the way you do. When there ain't nothin' to shoot at. Or be afeared of.'

Steele swung around easily to face the interior of the station. As the three men dropped down on to the hard chairs, Lorrimer and Parker looking eagerly at the open doorway to the old-timer's private quarters while Flynt continued to scowl at Steele.

'All life's surprises aren't pleasant ones, feller. I like to be ready.'

Bottles clinked together and tin cups rattled. Then Turner re-entered the room, awkwardly burdened with two bottles and five tin cups.

'Shame we ain't got somethin' else to celebrate. And celebrate with.' Lorrimer vented a sudden laugh as he and his companions took a cup each and held them out for Turner to fill them. 'Guess the westbound been through already, Bill?'

'Sure enough has, Dan. Late, but she's been through.'

The smell of unwashed men was strong in the hot shade of the way station. So that the aroma from the coffee pot in the other room was lost beneath it. But liquor went a little way to neutralise the unpleasant odour.

'Nothin' arrived for me, looks like,' Lorrimer said after a gulp at the rye whisky. 'The package Rocky told you you was to take care of for me.'

The bearded prospectors were no longer sweating after their fast ride out of the hills. But beads of salt moisture stood out on every pore of the old-timer's thin face as he extended a clean cup towards Steele.

The Virginian balanced his dirty coffee cup on top of it and said: 'Grateful to you, but I'm not a drinking man.'

'Rocky didn't say nothin' like that to me, Dan,' Turner answered huskily.

'When he brought the letter in last time,' Lorrimer reminded, some of the happiness gone from his tone. And he shared the start of a frown between the nervous Turner and the vacant-faced Parker. 'Package in the shape of a woman.' Now a grin of anticipation took command of his features. 'A female I ordered easy as pickin' out a new pair of boots from one of them fancy eastern catalogues.'

'I didn't know nothin' about that, Dan,' Turner insisted. And took a quick gulp of the whisky he had poured for himself.

Lorrimer glowered at the obviously dim-witted Parker for a stretched second. Then shook his head and fixed the grin back in place. 'Well, I guess it don't make no odds. You know about it now. And she sure ain't showed up yet. When she does, you take good care of her for me, you old bastard. But don't you do nothin' you shouldn't with her. I get first crack on account of it was my idea. Then Jay for writin' such pretty letters. And Rocky for bringin' them in to catch the stage. After that . . . well, you old bastard, I reckon we can work out a special cheap rate for you. You being so elderly, like. Not havin' such strong needs as the boys out in the hills.'

'I thank you, Dan,' Turner said. 'But I ain't never been with a whore since I got married and was widowed in the same year. Back in fifty-nine.'

'Miss Lucy Girard ain't no whore!' Lorrimer snarled, snatching up the unopened bottle from where Turner had placed it on a chair. Then smashing off the neck on the chair back and pouring whisky over the jagged edge into his cup. After he had taken a long swallow, the flare of anger was gone and he grinned again. 'Leastways, she won't be until after me and Jay and Rocky have had our fill of her.'

During the talk, while Parker enjoyed his liquor in small sips, Flynt did not drink at all. And transferred his suspicious attention from Steele to Bill Turner. Showed not even a flicker of surprise when Lucy Girard cried out in pain. Simply rasped: 'I friggin' knew it!'

'Shit!' Lorrimer snarled.

'A woman!' Parker growled.

Each man's voice competing with the others and with a thud, and the snort of a horse, from out front of the way station.

As Steele turned just his head. To see Lucy Girard spread-eagled on the trail. Beside the head-shaking gelding of Jay Flynt which had thrown her the moment she sat in the saddle.

'You sonofabitch!' Lorrimer yelled and it was as if his voice had a palpable force that drove Bill Turner back against the wall. As all three prospectors powered to their feet and lunged for the doorway, leaving trails of spilled liquor in their wakes. And Steele stepped easily outside, leaving them clear passage.

They skidded to a halt and stared in silence for long moments at the woman. Whose pained expression was replaced by deeply etched fear as she attempted to rise, but got no further than a sitting posture on the trail. Supporting the attitude with her hands in back of her on the ground: which served to emphasise the mounds of her breasts under the taut-stretched fabric of her gown.

Then Lucy moaned and it was like the sound made by a dog which knows from experience that it is to be whipped and there is no escape.

'Ain't she pretty?' Rocky Parker said in a reverential tone.

'As a friggin' picture,' Lorrimer agreed with a tremor in his voice.

'You picked the wrong horse, missy,' Jay Flynt growled. 'Mine don't let anyone ride him but me.'

The three men went towards her. Slowly. And the horse was more successful in backing off from them than the woman. She was still shaken and pained from the fall and her arms gave way. So that she collapsed out on to her back.

'Seems real eager to be took, don't she, Dan?' Parker said, and giggled.

But the sound of his glee was abruptly curtailed by a sound which brought him and the other two to a halt. The dry click of the Colt Hartford's hammer being cocked.

'Please,' Lucy Girard rasped with a dry sob.

But all three prospectors had swung their attention away from her. To glower over their shoulders at Adam Steele, who still had the rifle canted nonchalantly to his left shoulder.

'I friggin' knew it,' Flynt said again.

'You knew damn all, Jay,' Lorrimer snarled at him. Then: 'What interest you got in my woman, dude?'

'She asked me to help her, feller.'

'And how you gonna do that? Gun down three unarmed men?'

There were well worn, single-shot rifles in the boots hung from their saddles. Out of reach. And each had a knife in a sheath on his right hip.

'You don't look like the kind that gives nothin' for nothin', stranger,' Flynt accused.

Lucy Girard groaned in pain as she got to her feet.

Lorrimer glanced at her, then to Steele, and growled: 'You look like the kind that gets around a lot, dude. Gets to meet lots of willin' women all the time. What you want with her? Us and the rest of the boys out in the Dos Cabezas – we're lucky if we has female company more than once a year.'

Behind Steele, the floorboards creaked as Bill Turner moved away from the wall.

'You fellers chose your trade,' the Virginian drawled. 'Like for you to go out to back and bring my horse around, Miss Girard.'

'I surely will, and thank you so much, Mr Steele.'

She tried to run, but almost stumbled and so walked out of sight at the side of the way station, favouring her left leg. Parker watched her, disappointment etched deep into his fleshy face. While Lorrimer and Flynt continued to eye Steele with expanding hatred.

'Hell, Dan, give him the nugget for her, damnit!' Parker pleaded.

'She ain't his to sell, jughead!' the tallest of the three snarled. 'She's mine!'

'Ours!' Flynt corrected. 'And this pint-size friggin' dandy ain't gonna take her!'

He took a step forward, hands down at his sides so that his right was below the sheathed knife.

Steele straightened in the doorway as he arced the rifle away from his shoulder – bringing his right hand up to receive the barrel. So that the Colt Hartford was levelled from his hip, aimed at the belly of Jay Flynt. The threatened man froze, frightened by the cold glint that showed in the coal-black eyes of the Virginian.

A floorboard creaked. Immediately behind Steele. And Flynt started a grin of triumph. But the change of expression came too late for the Virginian. And he had time only to think about whirling around. Before the unmistakable shape of a gun muzzle put pressure on the base of his spine.

'Drop the rifle, sir,' Bill Turner ordered, and the fact that he had the drop on Steele did little to ease his anxiety. 'I don't go along with what Dan and his buddies plan for the lady. But better that than for three men I know to be shot down.'

'Atta boy, Bill!' Lorrimer snapped. 'Cheap rate nothin'! You get her for free, right after me!'

'While I'm makin' the dude wish he'd never stuck his nose in our business,' Jay Flynt growled, his grin of pleasure altering to one of viciousness.

'I'll go get her before she tries to steal *his* horse,' Parker said in high excitement.

And started around the corner of the way station as Lorrimer and Flynt moved in on Steele: advancing cautiously, as the Virginian chose to stoop and lower the rifle gently to the ground instead of allowing it to fall.

Steele did not think the prospectors intended to kill him. Certainly they were capable of killing a man, in blind rage or in self-defence. But they were not killers as such – in the way that he was able to take human life for any one of countless reasons. And still be able to sleep nights.

Nevertheless, he did not relish the prospect of the alternative which was implicit in the vicious expressions which shaped the features of Lorrimer and Flynt.

'Send him on his way is what should be done!' Bill Turner blurted as he saw the brute strength and intention to use it in the faces of the bearded men.

'You done fine, old man,' Lorrimer rasped. 'But that don't make you top man on the totem pole all of a sudden.'

The rifle was down on the ground and Steele seemed on the point of unfolding upright. Against the pressure of the old-timer's gun which had not been eased by his act of stooping. But, in the fraction of a second while Lorrimer and Flynt showed their scowls to the anxious Turner, the Virginian moved the Colt Hartford a fraction of an inch. To the right. Then squeezed the trigger. And powered his feet backwards.

21

The bullet cracked across a yard of air, raising dust with its slipstream from the ground an inch below its trajectory. Then blasted a hole in the toecap of Flynt's right boot. Forced a scream from his throat as it tore flesh from between two toes, cut a furrow along the sole of his foot and exited in a spray of blood from a point above the man's boot-heel.

Because he was injured on the right side, Flynt stumbled in that direction: falling hard against Lorrimer. Just as the old-timer fell equally hard on top of Steele — Turner's tumble caused by the force with which Steele's boots smashed into his ankles.

Steele heard the clatter of the old-timer's gun against the floor. But he did not see it. Jerked his body to dislodge Turner's light weighing frame off him and took a two handed grip on the rifle, gloved thumb cocking the hammer as he drew a bead on the crotch of Dan Lorrimer.

Lorrimer was a pace closer then, having shrugged off the clawing hands of Flynt who was now writhing on the ground, struggling to get his injured foot free of the boot.

'If I hear one move from the old-timer, you won't ever be able to have a woman again, feller.'

Lorrimer held still, except for moving both hands in front of Steele's target. Then swallowed hard before croaking: 'Do like he says, old man!'

'I think my arm's busted,' Turner moaned.

'I know my friggin' foot is!' Flynt snarled.

'Neither makes you any less of a man,' the Virginian drawled pointedly.

'Watch out!' Lucy Girard screamed. From around the corner of the way station where first she and then Rocky Parker had gone from sight. 'On the roof!'

The woman provided the warning with her cry. But an upward swivel of Lorrimer's eyes revealed the source of the threat before she put it into words. And Steele triggered a second shot against the sound of her voice. Having lunged over on to his back and angled the rifle upwards. Aiming at Parker who showed as just a dark silhouette against the bright blueness of the late morning sky. But despite the lack of detail about the man himself, it was clear to see that he was crouched on the rim of the roof in an attitude of hurling something downwards. Something metallic which glinted in the strong sunlight.

The bullet entered through the underside of Parker's jaw,

blasted a hole in his tongue and tunnelled up through the roof of his mouth before it came to rest in his brain, the deformed tip impacted against the inside of his skull. His head and torso were jerked upright by the force of the hit and the knife was thrown harmlessly to the side when his arms were spread. For a stretched second he teetered on the edge of the roof: then pitched down off it.

Steele, certain of a kill, had rolled over on to his belly by then. And started to get to his feet. Seeing that he was safe from attack by Dan Lorrimer. Who seemed rooted to the spot by horror as he stared up at the dying man, then followed the fast, limp-limbed descent of the corpse. While Jay Flynt, able to subdue his pain for a few moments, witnessed the same end to violence with much the same expression on his bearded face.

Dust billowed up around the body of the fat man. Began to settle.

The Virginian was on his feet, his cocked rifle canted to his shoulder. Cold eyes shifting from Lorrimer and Flynt to the ancient Bill Turner: who was also upright after his fall, standing on the way station threshold, apparently unaware of the Adams five-shot revolver on the floor a few inches from his left boot.

'You killed Rocky,' the old-timer accused, the huskiness of deep shock in his voice.

'No way I can deny it,' Steele drawled, feeling the tension drain from his muscles as he raked his eyes around the faces of the men again. Then shot a glance at Lucy Girard as the woman emerged from behind the corner of the way station and surveyed the scene across the backs of the two geldings still hitched to the hook.

'When he heard the shot and the man cry out, he just let go of me and climbed up on the roof,' she said, incredulity strong in her words.

'He always was a dumb sonofabitch,' Flynt growled.

'But the best friend we're ever likely to have,' Lorrimer added in deep melancholy. But his eyes when they shifted from the corpse to the Virginian expressed a deeper hatred.

'Save the eulogy for when you bury him, feller,' Steele said evenly.

'He was nothing more than a lusting animal!' the woman snapped, sharing her anger between Lorrimer and Flynt, who was again grimacing as he nursed his bloodied foot. 'The same

23

as you and you! Consider yourselves lucky you did not all die!'
Now she directed a contemptuous stare towards the abruptly
contrite old-timer in the doorway. 'You, too, Mr Turner! I
thought better of you! Yet when you saw an opportunity to
indulge your evil desires, you sided with these brutes against
this fine gentleman!'

The old man seemed helplessly lost for words for a stretched
second. Then, his remorse-filled eyes switching from the woman
to the Virginian and back, he muttered: 'You and Mr Steele
are strangers hereabouts, miss. Dan and his buddies, I known
them for a long time. Been good to me on occasions when they
hit paydirt. Figured it my duty to help them. I wouldn't have
done nothin' . . . wouldn't have took up the offer Dan
made . . .'

Now he was lost for words and he shook his head and
shrugged his skinny shoulders: defeated and despairing.

'Help me now, you old bastard!' Jay Flynt rasped through
gritted teeth. 'I need a belt for the pain and somethin' for my
foot to keep the gangrene from settin' in.'

'Reckon you should go finish the chore I gave you, ma'am,'
Steele said to the woman.

'Surely, surely,' she agreed and was suddenly drained by the
venting of her emotions. And there was a weariness in her gait
and bearing as she turned and went from sight at the side of the
way station.

As Turner came out of the building with a fresh bottle of
whisky. And Lorrimer moved to where Flynt sat on the trail
and stooped to help the groaning man up on to his uninjured
foot.

Steele also moved and stooped – to pick up Turner's revolver
and hurl it several yards out into the desert beyond the trail.
Then he got the woman's valise from where it stood in the
dust between the chair and the corpse of Rocky Parker. His
shadow falling across the body alarmed a horde of blood-
gorging flies away from the bullet-shattered head.

'She'll have to be real good to make it worth killin' for her,'
Lorrimer growled bitterly as Flynt snatched the bottle from
Turner and sucked at the neck.

'Killed on my own account, feller,' the Virginian answered
evenly as Flynt was moved gently towards the way station
doorway by his two helpers. 'It was either your partner or me.'

'A rifle-totin' gunslinger like you!' Jay Flynt snarled, spray-

24

ing droplets of whisky over his lips. 'You could've just winged him!'

Steele shifted a wry glance between the way station roof and the corpse, which was again providing food for desert flies. 'You reckon then he might have flown down, feller?'

Lorrimer spat, Flynt took another gulp from the bottle and the old-timer muttered about not knowing if he had anything for treating bullet wounds. As the three of them went in through the way station doorway. And Lucy Girard led Steele's black gelding out on to the trail.

'I take it, sir, that I may ride with you?' she asked, obviously relieved to see only the Virginian in front of the building. And taking a wide sweep around the fly-infested body of Parker.

Steele said nothing. He took the reins from her hand, slid the Colt Hartford into its boot and swung up across the saddle. Then, after hanging her valise from the horn, he reached down towards her. When she was astride the horse at his back, he said: 'Be a waste of effort if I left you here, ma'am. I'm headed north-east.'

She hooked her arms around him and interlocked her fingers at his belly. And a tremor moved her body against his as she said: 'Anywhere, Mr Steele. Anywhere away from here.'

Steele nodded and heeled the gelding forward at a slow walk. Not looking back. Not hearing any sounds from within the way station. Sensing the deep-seated animosity directed towards him and the woman, but certain Dan Lorrimer would not try to reach his horse, get the rifle from the boot and attempt to extract revenge for what had happened. Later, perhaps, after Parker had been buried and Jay Flynt's foot had healed. But not now, out on the open desert in the bright, broad sunlight: as an aggrieved gold prospector against a man who had shown himself to be a cool, merciless killer.

'I'm really glad there was a Southern gentleman like you around, Mr Steele,' the woman said after a long silence during which they rode a slow mile, she constantly glancing back towards the way station as it diminished in perspective. 'I'm from Mississippi myself and I'd say from your accent that you come from Virginia. Those lusting brutes – Yankees all of them!'

Her tone was calm until she referred to the men left back at the Way station.

'War's been over a long time, ma'am,' Steele answered coldly, and had a fleeting recollection of his brief partnership with a man named Edge.* 'Rebs and Yanks, they're all Americans now.'

He felt her move against his back and saw out of the corner of his eye that she was craning her neck to read the inscription engraved into the gold of the plate screwed to the stock of the Colt Hartford.

'It says to Benjamin P. Steele, with gratitude, Abraham Lincoln, ma'am,' he told her.

'Oh, so the fact that you are from Virginia . . . ? But, didn't you say your given name was Adam?'

'The gun belonged to my father.'

'Oh.'

There followed another long period of silence, as the sun moved beyond it's midday peak and the Gold Gulch way station was lost in the shimmering heat haze. Far ahead of the double riders, the dark, distant line of the Peloncillo Mountains seemed to get no closer.

'That horrible man Flynt was right about you, wasn't he?' Lucy said suddenly at length.

'What did he say?'

'That you were not much of a talker.'

'That why you advertised for a husband, ma'am? Because you wanted a man to talk to you?'

He felt her become tense against him as her encircling arms tightened. 'It's said the West is full of golden opportunities, Mr Steele,' she replied tautly. 'And if I ever had any of those back East, I certainly never took advantage of them.'

'East or West, nobody wins all the time.'

'I don't want heaven on earth. Just a fair crack of the whip, as they say.' This time it was not tension which caused her to embrace him more closely. 'And my luck certainly shone when you arrived back at that horrible place. Maybe your luck, too, if you will only unbend a little?'

'You reckon yourself some sort of prize, ma'am?' he countered evenly.

She wrenched her hands apart and tried to ride with them resting on her thighs. But then had to grip his hips to keep from sliding off the slow-moving horse.

'Sir, I would not have put myself up as such to just anybody!'

* *Edge and Steele: Two of a Kind.*

26

she snorted indignantly. 'And if you find my presence so disagreeable, please do not hesitate to stop the horse, put me down and hand me my valise.'

The Virginian pursed his lips and sighed. 'Reckon I can't do that, Miss Girard,' he said. 'Maybe it's the Southern gentleman in me that you talked about. But after what happened back at the way station, I consider I'm stuck with the situation. Bag and baggage.'

STEELE'S WAR
Book One

CHAPTER ONE

IT had been raining all that morning of April 16, 1861. A fine, mist-like Virginia rain that did not cool the air and caused tendrils of steam to rise from the fields of growing crops on the Steele Plantation. But shortly after midday the sun punched a hole in the greyness of the low sky and within an hour the clouds had rolled away to bank in the east.

The sun took this full sixty minutes to inch sufficiently across the sky so that it lanced through a dusty window of a storage barn to colour the eyelids of the couple who were sprawled out on top of a stack of cotton bales.

It was the girl who woke first, blinking; a perplexed expression on her pretty face. But even before she turned her head away from the sun's glare to see the young man beside her and then to look down at her upper body, she recalled where she was and how she had come to be there. And her smile at remembered pleasures expanded and became a peal of low laughter as she raised her back from the bales to sit up.

It was this sound of her joy in combination with the rays of the sun assaulting his eyelids which roused the man. Who took a little longer than her to collect his thoughts. But only because he had taken many more glasses of punch than she at last night's party in the big house. Which made memories elusive and sharp focus difficult in the first few seconds after waking.

'Why, I declare, Adam Steele,' the woman said in a tone of mock chiding. 'I do believe you don't recall what happened last night. And perhaps do not even remember who I am?'

He groaned as he eased up into a sitting position, and had to steady himself with his hands against the bales as the alcohol in his bloodstream threatened his sense of balance.

'Then you're wrong, honey,' he murmured with a broad,

slightly foolish grin. 'Because I know you're Miss Diana Summers. And last night I screwed the ass off of you. Two times. Slept in between.'

She laughed again. 'Well, I guess you know who I am right enough. But I bet you would not have recalled what happened if there were not all these clues around.'

The clues she spoke of were given by their state of undress. For she was entirely naked above the waist, the upper part of her low-cut, pale green gown unfastened at the back so that the bodice hung down, baring the shallow mounds of her dark, brown crested breasts. Her shoes, hose and white silk underthings were scattered to one side of her and the skirts of the gown were drawn up to display her slender legs below the knees.

Adam Steele's torso was also bare, his shirt, tie, vest and suit jacket hurriedly discarded along with his boots and hose. Some time he had yanked his pants back on, but they were still unbuttoned to a point where the narrow line of hair over his belly began to broaden.

'How could I forget?' he countered, allowing his bloodshot eyes to rove over the milky white, silken textured skin of her upper body. His tone was serious now. As earnest as the expression on his face.

The woman was quick to match his attitude with her own. 'Last night you said how easy it was to forget those Keysville whores you went with, Adam. And I thought –'

Steele was seated on her right. And he lashed at her with his left hand. A blow to her cheek with the backs of his extended fingers. That sent her sprawling on to her side with a cry of alarm as much as pain. Where she cowered in pathetic fear, her back and the entire length of one thigh exposed, looking up at his glowering face out of the corners of her tear-glistening eyes.

The flare of vicious temper was doused as suddenly as it had been ignited. 'God, I'm sorry, Diana,' he groaned, leaning to the side, hooking an arm around her shoulders and drawing her up beside him: using his free hand to press her reddened cheek to his shoulder. 'I shouldn't have done that. But promise me something, honey?'

'What, Adam?' she asked as her tears ran.

'Never talk of yourself in the same breath as those women who sell themselves in town.'

She buried her face in his shoulder and nodded, transferring the salt moisture from her flesh to his. Her voice was muffled when she said: 'If you promise me something as well, darling?'

'Just name it, honey?'

'That you'll never hit me again?'

She pulled away from him and tilted her head to look up into his face. Saw there for just part of a second the full depth of his remorse. Before the foolish grin swept it away.

'That's a real hard promise for me to make, Diana,' he told her. 'For I have it on good authority that it does a woman a world of good to be beaten every now and then. By her husband.'

His words took her breath away for long seconds. Then she closed and opened her eyes and worked her mouth to try to say something. Managed only: 'Oh, Adam!' before she threw her arms around him and collided with him so hard she knocked him over on to his back. Fell on top of him with her lips pressed to his.

It was a long, hard kiss of pure joy and excitement. That had just begun to become lingering and passionate when a fist hammered on the barn door. And a deep-throated voice yelled:

'Hey, Mister Adam, you inside there? You and Miss Diana both? Cause if you are, I sure hopes you is both decent!'

The woman sprang away from the man, a flush suffusing her face to mask the mark made by the back-handed blow.

'Don't you dare come in here, Elroy!' she shrieked, fumbling to catch hold of the gown bodice and yank it up in front of her breasts. Then she scrambled to her feet, her embarrassment at the interruption mixed with chagrin at the sight and sound of Adam Steele's laughter. 'You must not come in one second before I call that you can. You hear?'

She had tried to fix the back fastenings of the gown, but been unable to manage it. Then had thudded back down to the cotton bales and presented an illustration of more haste meaning less speed as she struggled to get into her underthings.

'I hears you, Miss Diana!' the Negro foreman of the Steele Plantation responded. 'And I guesses I can waits as long as it takes.'

'I just wish to fix my hair is all, Elroy.'

'Yes, Miss Diana,' Elroy responded with obvious disbelieving good humour.

'Mr Adam had a trifle too much punch last evening and I

brought him outside the house for some fresh air!' Breathlessly as she pulled on her hose.

'Yes, Miss Diana.'

'It's the absolute truth, Elroy!'

Standing up now, trying to push her feet into turned-over shoes while working on the gown fastenings again. Glowering down at Steele who continued to grin as he got dressed with slow deliberation.

'Yes, Miss Diana.'

'He felt ill and we came in here! Where he passed out! Then I began to feel a trifle dizzy and lay down!'

'Yes, Miss Diana.'

Fully dressed except for his vest and suit jacket, Steele rose, stepped up behind the woman and gently moved her hands away so that he was able to fasten the gown bodice. 'Least one thing you told Elroy was the truth, honey,' he whispered in her ear.

She interrupted her sigh of relief to gasp: 'Uh?'

'That we came in here.' He brushed his lips across the fading mark of the blow on her cheek. And her embarrassment was ended by a fit of giggling as he swung her around and they looked at each other with laughing eyes.

She was twenty-one years old. A five-feet, three-inches tall brunette, her dark hair long enough to spill down and brush the upper curves of her breasts. This after framing an oval-shaped, evenly tanned face. Her eyes were large and brown, her nose had an attractive upward tilt at the tip and her mouth was full and slightly pouted. She had retained a perfect complexion from childhood and she had no need of rouge and powder.

Adam Steele was three years older than Diana and a little over three inches taller. With a build that was in proportion to his height: lean rather than thin, the flesh hard-packed and the skin rough-textured. A body that had been developed by hard work around the plantation and a love of tough outdoor pursuits during periods of relaxation. An adult man's body then – with which his face was a little at odds. It was a nondescriptly handsome face, the skin tanned but with few lines yet. And he did not have to shave more than three times a week. The construction of his features was regular but undistinguished, forming a face that would not stand out in a crowd. Except if one took into account his neatly clipped hair which for several years had been in the slow process of turning from auburn to premature grey. A transformation that in low lighting could make him look considerably older than his years. Just as the foolish grin which turned up the corners of his gentle mouth-line and put a sparkle in his coal-black eyes acted to make him look like a callow adolescent.

'Twice,' Diana reminded. 'And I promise I'll get better.'

'You learn real fast,' he said and they kissed again. Then, when it was over and he turned to jump down to the dirt floor, she rubbed unsuccessfully with a shoe sole the bloodstain on the cotton bale: which marked the spot where she had sur-rendered her virginity to the man she loved. Next allowed her-self to be lifted down by the compact, easy strength of Steele.

'Is it all right to come in, Miss Diana?' Elroy called. His voice louder now, to be heard above the clop of hooves and sound of turning wheelrims.

'Yes, you may come now,' the woman allowed, brushing at her creased gown with both hands. Then screwing up her eyes against the flood of bright sunlight that entered the barn with the opening of the big doors.

'Afternoon to you, Miss Diana, Mr Adam. Sure has turned out to be a fine day after the rain, ain't it?'

Elroy wore just a dirty pair of white pants. No shirt, shoes or hat. He was a giant of a man, standing six inches taller than six feet and weighing close to two hundred and fifty pounds. His build was muscular and there was a great strength of character visible in his round and shiny face under the cap of tightly curled hair. He was somewhere in his early fifties – he was not sure exactly – and only when his features were in repose was it possible to see in them telltale signs of long years of suffering. Mostly though, since he had been bought by Ben Steele and gained rapid promotion over six years to achieve foreman, Elroy smiled. And the lines of this expression at the corners of his eyes and mouth were the most prominent.

'It's afternoon?' Diana exclaimed. 'Goodness, Adam, we've been asleep all that time!'

'Yes, miss,' the Negro confirmed. And curtailed a laugh to add: 'Time which could've been better spent practisin' how to fix up your hair. Wouldn't you say, Mr Adam?'

He continued the interrupted laugh and slapped his thigh. As Steele grinned, both men watching the woman's consternation as she raised her hands to her head. To explore the tangled disarray of the tresses which she had claimed was the reason Elroy was forced to wait outside.

Then she was gripped by another fit of the giggles and clung to Steele's arm: the three of them standing on the threshold of the barn. As a line of four flatbed wagons came to a halt outside, two smiling Negroes up on each seat.

'Mr Ben says to ship all the bales outta here down to the railroad station for the ten-o'clock freight,' Elroy reported, abruptly assuming a slave-master attitude. Jealous of the easy-going relationship he enjoyed with the Steele father and son in private and ever anxious that the other slaves who worked the plantation should not share in it. 'But I can handle it, Mr Adam. If you got other things to do.'

Steele shook his head. 'Reckon I'll stay, feller. Some heavy work is just what I need to get over too much punch and too long sleeping. Take these for me, honey?'

He handed his suit jacket and vest to Diana.

'What I need is a bath and to wash my hair. I'll see you at dinner?'

'Reckon so,' he answered, rolling up his sleeves as, at a signal from Elroy, the Negroes climbed down from the wagons.

'You'll tell father tonight?' the woman whispered to Steele as she took his unwanted clothes.

'And I'll tell yours and mine to delay the celebration for awhile. Or at least to count me out if they want to seal it with liquor.'

He watched her for a few moments as she started off along the gravel driveway, passing the line of halted wagons, heading back for the big house: the red tile roof and white-faced chimneys could be seen above the tops of the trees which screened most of the Colonial-style building from this direction. Then he swung around to start doing his share of the muscle-straining labour involved in transferring the stored cotton bales on to the wagons.

Certainly Ben Steele and John Summers would demand that there be a lavish party to celebrate the engagement of their son and daughter. A party that would be on a much grander scale than that of the previous evening – which had been staged simply because two of the richest cotton and tobacco growers in Virginia felt like marking the end of a highly profitable year.

The Summers plantation was on the other – eastern – side of the small railroad town of Keysville and Adam and Diana had known each other since childhood as a result of their fathers' friendship. From far back, there had always been hope that the children might one day themselves become more than mere friends. And then from their mid-teens hope had been transformed into assumption.

For awhile, such an attitude by their respective fathers had acted to alienate the youngsters – against their elders and each other. But this natural youthful rebelliousness was later negated by mutual attraction. Which had reached physical culmination last night in the storage barn where Steele now sweated and grunted among the near-naked Negro slaves as he helped to load the wagons.

To the majority of whites – from those as rich and privileged as the Steeles and the Summers to the redneck sharecroppers – who lived in the southern states, such a scene would have been anathema. Just as the earlier good-humoured confidences shared by the white couple and Elroy would have aroused contempt and even furious hatred in such people.

Surreptitiously in the Keysville area, where many depended for their livelihoods upon the Steele and Summers plantations, the widower fathers and their only children were called nigger lovers. While further afield the taunts were voiced openly. But Ben Steele and John Summers had always treated their slaves well: more so than ever since the Dred Scott Decision of the Supreme Court in the March of 1857 which declared that Negroes were not United States citizens and were to be classed as chattels of their masters.

Wealth and the power which came with it enabled the plantation owners to maintain their policy and remain aloof from the criticisms directed at them. But political events were making this increasingly difficult.

Just a few months ago, at the end of last year and the opening of the new, South Carolina, Mississippi, Florida, Alabama, Georgia, Louisiana and Texas had seceded from the Union: with slavery as a major issue in the momentous decision. Then, within a two-week span in February, at Montgomery Alabama, a Confederate States of America was formed and Jefferson Davis was nominated and inaugurated as president.

Now it was mid-April, with the newly elected President Abraham Lincoln installed in Washington and rumours of imminent civil war were rife. There had been a great deal of war talk among the men in the library after dinner last night, sparked by the news on good authority that a Confederate artillery barrage had begun to be laid into Fort Sumter, South Carolina three days previously.

Had not Adam Steele decided at the start of the party that this would be the night upon which he relieved Diana of her maidenhood, he might have taken more of an interest in the discussion. Joined his father and John Summers and the dozen or so other men in talk of peace and war, American and world opinion, the merits of Lincoln and Davis and so on. But he had been unable to shift from his alcohol-fuzzed mind an image of Diana, her alluring smile and the way her breasts bunched above the low neckline of her ball gown. So it had been with great relief that he greeted the conclusion of the brandy and cigar interlude and the men joined the ladies for dancing or bridge or simply conversation on less serious subjects. A relief that approached ecstasy when, after drinking too much punch, his implied proposition to Diana was eagerly accepted.

And he took her – she a willing novice and he experienced from the professional services provided by the house in Keysville.

While he worked at the loading chore, he thought only of the pleasures of her body: and was sure that if he had not been engaged in such hard labour he would have become aroused again. Then, when a rest was called and four black women brought coffee and lemonade, he listened only vaguely to the joking talk of the slaves as he reflected upon the marriage proposal he had made. That had been entirely impulsive – certainly it had not been considered as a part of his preconceived plan to possess the woman. Either as an encouragement for her submission or a reward for it.

But he discovered he had no regrets. And he smiled as he sat on the grass, his back against the trunk of a live oak beside the barn. Relishing the prospect of marriage to Diana: his anticipation of the estate due only in small part to the fact that it would provide him with constant access to her firm, athletic body.

'I ain't so sure you ain't laced that coffee with somethin' stronger, Mr Adam,' Elroy said, breaking in on Steele's train of thought.

'What's that, feller?'

'You's smilin' like you is king of the world,' the foreman augmented as the other Negroes began to move back to their labours. 'Or is it maybe you had such a good time with – '

'Shut your filthy mouth, mister!' Steele snarled, powering to his feet and hurling away his empty coffee cup as he glared up into the abruptly perplexed face of the much taller man.

The rest of the slaves who had been moving slowly back to work suddenly moved faster: pretending they had not heard the harsh-spoken words or seen Steele's enraged expression.

The younger Steele's potentiality for switching from easy good humour into vicious rage was well known far and wide. And on the whole was accepted by most as his single bad fault – remarkable that he should have just the one, many thought, for a young man who had been over-indulged and spoiled from the day he was old enough to desire luxuries and be granted them.

For the most part, those who came into close personal contact with Adam Steele made the conscious effort to steer clear of subjects which they knew or merely guessed might trigger his bad temper. But on occasions, such as with Diana earlier and Elroy now, an innocent remark was likely to ignite his anger.

'I'm sorry, Mr Adam,' the giant Negro gulped, contrition carved deep into his shiny, sweat-beaded face. 'I didn't knows I was speakin' outta turn, sir.'

Sometimes Steele's rage went so deep he was unable to control it without opening the safety valve of physical action. As with Diana Summers. At other times he was able to keep a finger-hold on reason for long enough to realise that he and not the other person was wrong. As now.

'Shit, it's me that's sorry, Elroy,' he said, venting the words on a stream of pent-up breath. 'How the hell can you read my mind?'

'I can't, Mr Adam.'

'And neither can any of the other men over at the black quarters, feller.' He showed his foolish grin but the Negro unbent only so far as to become impassive. 'Like for you to tell them. The women, too. But not until tonight.'

'Tell them what, Mr Adam?'

Steele stopped grinning. 'Miss Diana and me, Elroy. I reckon all of you people have been watching me stalk her.'

'You ain't made no secret of it, sir.'

'Sure. But now it's different.'

The Negro started to grin. 'You mean . . . ? You and Miss Diana, you got plans?'

Steele nodded and the grin on Elroy's face expanded to a

wide beam .'Right, feller. She isn't just a piece of ass any more. She's my intended. You tell them that, uh?'

He bunched his right hand into a fist and raised his own grin again as he directed a half-power punch against Elroy's flat, muscle-rippling belly.

'I'll be right proud to do that, Mr Adam,' the big black man said excitedly. 'Tonight after supper. And if I hears any of my people speakin' outta line about you and Miss Diana, I'll kick their butts from here to the Potomac. And the last kick I gives them'll send them skimmin' all the way back to Africa.'

The white man and the Negro went back into the barn to resume work and met with no curious glances from the slaves who were already toting bales between the diminishing piles and the laden wagons. For, just as Adam Steele was notorious for his quick temper, it was also known that he was able to recover his composure just as readily. And be generous if he admitted to being in the wrong.

'It's a marriage lots of my people have always hoped for, Mr Adam,' Elroy said softly as he and Steele hefted the final cotton bale on to the back of the last wagon in the line. 'And one I been expectin' to be made.'

The white man matched the black one's grin as he replied: 'That's fine, feller.' He glanced into the now empty barn, murky since the afternoon sun had slid across the sky and no longer shone inside. 'But keep your fingers crossed nothin' else is expected.'

CHAPTER TWO

THE four wagons were turned around on an open area out back of the barn while Steele and Elroy checked through the shipment papers and the white man signed that the bale tally was correct. Then, as the wagons were halted so that the foreman could climb up on to the seat of the first one, hoofbeats sounded on loose gravel. The animals being galloped from the south – as yet out of sight of the men in front of the empty barn – along a wagon track between a row of leaf-drying sheds and several acres of growing tobacco, were not seen until the riders reined in their mounts at the intersection of the track and driveway which curved from the plantation's main gateway in the east boundary fence to the big house at the centre of the Steele property.

There were six of them, well known to Adam Steele either as former classmates in school and college or because they worked in various businesses in Keysville.

The bespectacled Cornell Banning and the brightly ginger-haired Brewster Davidson were of an age with Steele and he had known them the longest. The beefily built Cliff Gordon was two years older and the son of the railroad depot manager. Conrad Shotter, squint-eyed and squat, helped his parents run the Keysville House Hotel. He was not yet twenty. Just past their majority were Andrew Harding and Nicholas Kane: the former a tall and thin, mild-mannered young man who worked in the haberdashery store owned by his widowed mother and the latter fat to the point of obesity – a would-be writer who covered weddings, funerals and social events for the *Keysville Chronicle* which was edited by his father.

'Hey, Adam!' Banning yelled. 'Have you heard the news?'

His voice was slurred. And Shotter and Harding almost slid

from their saddles as all the horses were jerked around to be cantered along the driveway towards the head of the wagon line. Davidson wore a stupid grin and Kane looked pale and ready to be sick. Only Cliff Gordon appeared not to have been drinking. But he was well known as a hard drinker for his age and was probably holding his liquor better than the rest. He remained at the rear of the group, a glower on his face, as the horses were reined in.

'About Sumter, buddy,' Davidson augmented as Steele surveyed the young men quizzically. 'It's fallen!'

'That's right, Adam,' Banning cut in, making an effort to keep his words distinct. 'Two days ago. Major Anderson surrendered to General Beauregard and Charleston's gone crazy. It's war now.'

'Grateful for the trouble you took to let me know, fellers,' Steele said, and handed the shipment papers up to Elroy who – like the rest of the Negroes on the wagons – was suddenly frowning anxiously.

'I told you guys we'd be wastin' our time comin' out here,' Cliff Gordon growled. 'Steele ain't never been nothin' but a friggin' chip off the old block!'

'That's not true!' Brewster Davidson countered, whirling in his saddle to scowl at the big-built Gordon. While the other mounted men saw Steele stiffen and grimace in response to the taunt as he turned from the wagon seat. 'Adam is – '

'His Pa's son,' Gordon finished, calm in face of Brewster's defensive anger. And clucked his horse forward, forcing a way to the front of the group. Where he dropped the reins and folded his arms across his broad chest. 'Look at him now. Sweatin' as much as the nigras. On account of he's been workin' with them. Just like him and them are the same.'

'Cut it out, Cliff,' Andy Harding urged anxiously.

'You shut your Goddamn mouth!' Gordon snarled, his anger rising to match the level of that which had gripped Steele. He glanced only fleetingly at the skinny store clerk before returning his intense gaze to the prematurely grey man beside the lead wagon. 'Reason we left Keysville was to go enlist in the army of the Confederate States of America. Which means we're fixin' to smash the nigra-lovin' Union and anyone else who ain't for us. And I don't see no reason why we got to wait until we got us uniforms to start.'

42

'We'll leave, Adam,' Cornell Banning offered, and made to turn his horse.

'Not yet we don't!' Gordon snarled, and kicked free of both stirrups, swung one leg over the neck of his horse and slid from the saddle. 'I wasn't for comin' out here to this stinkin' rich place! But now you dragged me out here, I ain't gonna make it a wasted journey! War's started so Steele money don't mean a Goddamn anymore!'

'Easy, Mr Adam,' Elroy urged as Steele started forward alongside the team of the lead wagon.

'Hear that?' Gordon growled, and vented a harsh laugh as he swung his head to look at the mounted men. 'These stinkin' rich nigra-lovin' sonsofbitches even let the bastard slaves tell them what to do!'

As a result of his regret at striking Diana and the pangs of conscience he felt over the close call with Elroy, Steele had been able to keep his temper in check for longer than usual in face of Gordon's goading diatribe. But now he reached his limit. And lunged towards the bigger man, a silent snarl drawing his lips back from his teeth and putting glints in his dark eyes.

'Cliff!' Nick Kane shrieked, jerking on his reins to move his horse to the side.

Gordon snapped his head around. And grinned. Having ample time to ready himself for the frantic attack as Steele closed the ten feet gap between them.

His whole being suffused by the white heat of an all-consuming rage, Adam Steele could think of nothing beyond making painful contact with his antagonist. And he paid the price for his foolish impetuosity.

For Cliff Gordon stood his ground until the last part of a second and then, with perfect timing, side-stepped: leaned away from Steele's flailing fists and raised a knee.

Steele took the kneecap in the crotch, doubled over and felt every joint in his body explode with agony as he was brought to a jarring halt. As his head slammed into the hindquarter of Gordon's wheeling horse. He went down hard to the driveway, feeling a different brand of pain as sharp-cornered gravel dug into his hands and the side of his head. Heard other areas of the gravel crunch as the mounted men backed away from the immediate scene of the fight astride nervous horses.

'That's right, nigra-lover!' Gordon taunted. 'Stay down there and eat dirt! Cause that's what all you cock-suckers of Abe Lincoln'll be doin' soon as this war gets started for real!'

'Let's go, Cliff!' Conrad Shotter yelled. 'You made your point!'

Steele rolled over on to his back and vented a sound for the first time since he lunged into the impulsive attack. He groaned his pain. As he stared up at the cloudless blue sky above the plantation. A moment later saw a part of the sky obstructed by the towering form of Gordon.

'Seems like I surely did,' the man responsible for Steele's pain and humiliation crowed. 'Too damn easy for my likin'. So I reckon I might just go up to the money-stinkin' house. Way I hear it the nigra-lovin' Summers are still there. The old men'll be easier than you to take, I reckon. Then maybe I'll have me some kinda reward. With that small-tit snotnose Summers girl. Show her a white man can give her a hell of a better time than the buck nigras she's been lettin' screw her until now. Spoils of war, I reckon it's called.'

It was Gordon who had made the mistake this time. Too intent upon enjoying premature triumph by heaping insults on his victim to be aware that Steele was using suffering to cool his hot anger. And the time of taunting to summon up reserves of energy.

'Quit it, Cliff!' Harding snapped. 'He's beat. And that kind of talk isn't getting us where we want to go!'

'It ain't just friggin' talk!' Gordon snarled, shifting his hard-eyed gaze to the usually quiet-voiced store clerk. 'I'm tellin' it the way I figure to do it!'

The five mounted men, sobered by what had happened, were abruptly shocked: convinced that Gordon meant what he said. The Negroes, still seated rigidly on the wagon seats, were equally certain of this. And some of them closed their eyes and moved their lips in silent prayer.

Until Cliff Gordon vented a shrill cry of alarm. This as Steele rolled on to his side, curled an arm around the bigger man's lower legs and thudded his shoulder into the kneecaps.

Taken completely by surprise, his triumphant gaze still fixed on the terrified black men when Steele started the move, Gordon was unbalanced and fell backwards. Body stiff and arms flailing at thin air. Until he crashed to the gravel on his back, the cry of fear changing note to signal pain.

With his face run with blood on one side, Steele retained his grip on Gordon's legs as he drew himself up on to his knees and then got to his feet.

For a moment, Gordon was stunned by his head slamming into the gravel and winded by the impact of his back against the ground. And was defenceless as Steele, his temper rising and growing hot again, twisted the legs to turn his opponent over on to his face.

'You bastard!' Gordon shrieked, and made to press his hands to the ground and jerk his ankles free of Steele's grip.

But he was a fraction of a second too late in his recovery and attempted counter. For Steele had already made his next move – powering into an awkward but fast backward run. Causing the already nervous horses further distress. So that the animals shifted out of his path without commands from their riders. As Steele dragged the cursing and struggling Cliff Gordon face down along the driveway.

For a few staggering backward steps, Gordon's attempts to free himself got stronger. But this served only to harden Steele's resolve to hold on to his victim and make him suffer.

Gordon's curses gave way to howls of pain as the sharp edges of gravel ripped the fabric of his shirt and then lacerated the skin of his chest and belly.

Steele had dragged the bigger and heavier man beyond the divided bunch of horses and riders now. And felt the expression on his blood-and-sweat-run face alter from grimacing hatred to a brutal grin as he heard his victim give vent to a greater pain than he felt. Then, a few moments later, found fresh reserves of strength when he saw the blood of Gordon show on the gravel.

'I'll teach you, you bastard!' he shrieked, throwing his head back to stare at the sky again, the veins standing out like blue ropes under the skin of his throat.

As he came to a halt and was able to swing Gordon clear of the ground as he whirled. The man moaned, then curtailed the sound as he slammed down, face on to the gravel this time.

Steele heard voices shouting. Just a babble of noise, as he recommenced his backward run – towards the head of the line of wagons now. Began to discern words against the crunch of gravel under his feet.

'Adam!'

'Mr Adam, no!'

'Steele, you'll kill him!'

45

'He's done for!'

Steele felt the strength grow inside him – as if the more energy he expended, the greater his capability became. And then he was gripped by a light-headed sense of great power: this triggered by the wider trail of blood left by the unconscious form of Cliff Gordon. The bright crimson spilled from the jaw and side of the head and the limply dragging hands as well as the belly and chest.

Ecstatic joy drove reality far back beyond the seemingly impenetrable walls of cruel fantasy. There was just himself and this bleeding thing at his mercy within this dream world. And he could not even remember who or what was bleeding. Or why he was impelled to go on making it suffer.

Then the contact he had with his victim seemed suddenly too remote. The bleeding thing was a man who he was gripping merely by the ankles. So he halted the run, hurled aside the legs and powered into a crouch: saw the blood on his own hands as he heaved Gordon over on to his back.

Gordon was unrecognisable because of the bright, bubbling, gravel-littered redness which sheened his face.

Voices continued to shout at him. Not so loudly as before. As if the people yelling were backing off. But it only sounded that way in his mind.

He straddled the blood-run belly of Gordon and raised an arm to launch a punch at the pulped face. Sensed rather than saw a massive shadow fall across him. Felt his raised arm caught in a powerful grip around his wrist.

'No more, Mr Adam,' a voice said softly. Very close.

A stab of reason penetrated into Steele's private world of unreasoning hatred. And he looked up and around. Saw it was the anxious faced Elroy who held his arm. Beyond him saw the terrified Negroes on the wagons. Glanced over his shoulder and recognised the men astride horses, some showing shock and others looking like they were going to be sick. Then he recalled the identity of the man beneath him and the events which had preceded this situation.

'Let go of me, you big black bastard!' he rasped.

'Adam!' a familiar voice roared.

As Steele wrenched his arm free and Elroy staggered backwards, spun away. He launched the punch. But it never connected, for he froze in an instantaneous reaction to a gunshot:

46

that exploded a bullet which kicked up gravel six inches away from his bent right knee.

A wave of pain broke over him, touching every part of him. Caused as much by the massive expending of energy as by the crashing fall with which the contest had begun.

'Easy, pal,' a second well-known voice urged.

Steele turned his head to the side, fighting back the bile which threatened to swamp his throat and trigger vomit. His eyes were moist and the two men at the edge of the driveway were indistinct. But even in such circumstances, Steele was able to recognise his father and his best friend.

It was the lanky and lean Jim Bishop who had fired the shot, the revolver in his hand still wisping smoke from the muzzle. The metal of the gun did not gleam so brightly in the late afternoon sunlight as the deputy's badge pinned to his shirt front.

The sixty-year-old, short and slightly built Ben Steele stood beside the lawman, reaching out an arm to touch his hand to Bish's shoulder.

'Get him, Elroy,' the elder Steele snapped.

As the younger one succeeded in holding back the vomit. But began to topple to the side. Was prevented from slamming into the gravel again by the strength of the big black man hooking hands under his armpits. Then raising him to his feet: and keeping him upright with an arm around his middle – as easily as a mother might support a young child.

'Now what in God's name has been happening here?' Ben Steele demanded, fixing a hard stare on the group of mounted men.

Several of them hung their heads while others cleared their throats. Adam Steele's head was already hanging, chin resting on his chest. But he fought to raise it and to speak before anyone else answered.

'Personal, Pa,' he croaked. 'Between Cliff Gordon and me.'

'Joshua, Luke!' Ben Steele said grimly and two Negroes leapt down from a wagon. 'Pick up the other boy and bring him up to the house. Elroy, you see that Mr Adam –'

'No, sir!' Brewster Davidson cut in after glancing to left and right and seeing that nobody else was about to intervene. 'Cliff wouldn't thank you for it.'

'I'm not looking for gratitude, young man!' the elder Steele countered.

Davidson swung down from his horse and after a moment of hesitation, Shotter and Banning followed his example. The three of them advanced to where Gordon lay sprawled in front of Adam Steele and Elroy.

'We're on our way to join the army of the Confederate States, sir,' Davidson explained, and gestured for Shotter and Banning to pick up the unconscious man. 'Guess you've heard Sumter has surrendered and the Yankees are pulling out of Virginia. Burning everything that might be of help to the CSA.'

'I am aware of that, young man,' Ben Steele said tensely, restraining Jim Bishop as Gordon was raised from the damaging gravel and carried to his horse. 'But that is no reason why that hurt boy should suffer unnecessarily – '

'Beg pardon, sir,' Davidson interrupted. 'Some of us thought Adam might wish to volunteer with us. Cliff didn't want to come. When he got here, he made trouble. Insulted your family and the Summers, sir. Reckon he'll hurt real bad on the way to enlist. But the way his mind works, it would be worse for him if he woke up in your house. Like to leave now, sir. With your permission.'

'War may not come,' Ben Steele said, addressing the opinion to all the horsemen as Davidson remounted.

'You and your kind hope,' Conrad Shotter muttered.

'Adam?' Cornell Banning called.

The younger Steele turned his gravel-scratched, pain-wracked face towards his old schoolmate.

'You were right about this being personal between you and Cliff. If you want to join us now or later, there won't be any hard feelings from the rest of us.'

Heads were nodded in agreement.

'The same with me, fellers,' Adam said.

He extricated himself gently from Elroy's support. But moved only a half-pace away from the big black man. And his father's anxious frown was replaced by an expression of relief.

'How about you, Bish?' Andy Harding asked the young deputy sheriff. 'You got no love for Yankees, have you?'

'Law has to be maintained and it can't work unless it's impartial,' Jim Bishop said evenly and without pomposity.

There were nods of acceptance rather than agreement. Then the men turned their horses and rode them slowly along the drive, Banning and Davidson flanking the mount of Gordon with hands stretched to the side to hold the unconscious man in place across his saddle.

'Where are you headed?' the younger Steele called after them, his grimace of physical pain matched by an expression of anguish on the face of his father.

'Richmond,' Andy Harding answered. 'Nick's Pa says Virginia's going to secede any time now. And Richmond will be the Confederate capital.'

'You should get that boy to Doctor Graves before you go anywhere!' Ben Steele shouted after the departing group.

There was no response and the riders kept their backs firmly towards the men left behind on the driveway.

Ben Steele sighed and gestured for Elroy and the other Negroes to climb back up on the wagons.

'Is there gonna be a war, Mr Ben?' one of the young slaves sharing the seat with Elroy asked, and refused to meet the withering stare of the foreman.

The impeccably dressed, compact-built Ben Steele looked suddenly much older than his sixty years as the lines in his weathered, kindly face deepened in a frown. 'There already is, Joshua,' he answered. Then made a visible effort to alter his mood of depression. 'But until we know the precise situation, it's important we carry on as normal. And right now we need to get these bales to the depot.'

'Yes, sir,' Elroy responded, took the reins and cracked them over the backs of the team.

Adam Steele stepped back painfully out of the path of the wagon line, on the opposite side of the driveway from his father and Jim Bishop. Then, when the last wagon had rolled by, he tried hard not to let his pain show as he crossed to join them.

'You need a doctor, son?' his father asked.

'Be fine after I've washed up. How you been, Bish?'

'Okay, until I heard the same news as everyone else in Keysville. Then heard some ugly talk. Of the kind I guess that started the fight between you and Cliff Gordon. The sheriff rode out to warn Mr Summers and I came to tell your Pa. Should be getting back to town now.'

'Grateful to you, son,' Ben Steele said.

'Do me a favour, Bish?' Adam asked.

'Name it.'

'Diana's up at the house. She was going to stay a few days.

Grateful if you'd take her home for me.' He gestured with his hands in front of himself. 'Before she sees me like this.'

Jim Bishop nodded.

'Or hears your plans and tries to talk you out of them?' Ben Steele said grimly.

'I haven't made any plans!' his son countered sharply.

'Plans are born of ideas. And you have one of those in your head, sure enough.'

Bishop swung his head to and fro between the father and son, looking uncomfortable. 'What'll I tell her, Adam?' he asked, obviously anxious to leave before the family argument developed further.

The younger Steele felt the hot flare of new anger in his belly. Directed at Jim Bishop for not doing his own thinking – forcing him to turn his mind away from a more important problem. But he conquered the emotion.

'Hell, I don't know.' Then, after a moment's pause: 'Tell her I went to town with the wagons. And with the war rumours so strong, I think it best she should be with her Pa.'

'Sure thing, Adam.' The youthful, pleasant-faced deputy swung away.

'I'll go with him, son,' Ben Steele said. 'See you in awhile. After you've had time to do some serious thinking. Unless you want to wait until after you feel better?'

The older man was obviously concerned about his son – as anxious about his physical condition as the divided loyalties that had put his mind in a turmoil. Recognising this, Adam sought to lighten the mood and showed his foolish grin as he replied: 'I'm all right, Pa. Feeling a little stiff is all. Just have to make sure I don't act like a big one.'

CHAPTER THREE

ADAM Steele went to bed early that night in his large, luxuriously furnished room on the second floor of the big house. He made the excuse that he needed a long sleep to speed his recovery from the effects of the fight with Cliff Gordon. He even had dinner sent up on a tray.

But he ate hardly any of the food and the many clocks in the house had struck one in the morning before he finally subsided into sleep. After long, dragging hours of carefully considered mental debate. Which served to take his mind off his physical discomforts but from which he reached no conclusive decision.

Ben Steele did not question his son's early-to-bed tactic and on the next bright morning, over breakfast the father made no mention of the events of the previous afternoon. But it was not a silent meal. Rather, the routine business conference it always was on ordinary days: as the two Steeles reviewed what was necessary to keep the plantation running efficiently until nightfall.

Ben Steele, with the advantage of many more years of experience, proved to be the better actor: expertly maintaining the pretence that this day was just like any other. And even helping out his son when Adam's façade of normalcy looked in danger of cracking.

It was agreed that the son should supervise the ploughing of a ten-acre field at the north-west corner of the plantation which had lain fallow for a year. While the father rode a buggy into town to deal with business matters at the bank. The charade came closest to collapse on this point for both men were aware that business at the bank had all been neatly tied up only last week.

But the meal and the talk was over by then, so both were able to leave the white linen-covered table set with silver and bone china and go their separate ways.

Adam Steele spent a long, hot day in the ten-acre field and did more than his fair share of the heavy manual labour which was needed to prepare the rested soil for a new crop of tobacco.

Elroy had driven Ben Steele into Keysville, but it was obvious that he spoke in strong terms to the other slaves before he left. All but the most dull-witted of them were seething with questions: and finding it difficult to contain their anxious curiosity. Particularly since the white man in their midst was normally ready to talk to them and help whenever there was a problem.

When the preoccupation with his personal dilemma was briefly interrupted by trouble with a skittish horse pulling one of the ploughs, Steele became aware of the tension around him. Saw the tacit questions in the anxious eyes of the Negroes. Realised that Elroy must have warned them not to voice their doubts unless invited to do so. And wondered if his father had instructed Elroy to do this.

He said: 'All I can tell you is that there's sure to be a war. Mr Ben's in town now and maybe when he gets back, he'll have more to tell you. But something you can be sure of. Whatever happens, he'll do the best he can for you people and your families.'

The assurance put into words acted to ease the minds of several men who, like every slave on the plantation, had never doubted that they would be protected to the best of Ben Steele's ability.

'And you, Mr Adam?' Luke posed tentatively, the query causing all eyes to gaze again into the temporarily scarred face of the white man.

A face which seemed on the point of expressing a frown of rising anger: so that several Negroes backed off from where Steele stood beside the now calm horse. But he quelled the emotion and pursed his lips to vent a sigh: knowing that the men were just as concerned about his fate as their own.

'You'll hear that from Mr Ben or from me,' he said evenly. 'Depending upon what I plan to do. Now, let's get back to work, uh?'

Ben Steele did not return to the big house until after dinner. Wet from the rain which looked set to fall all night. Barely

52

polite to the servants who felt he should eat even though he said he was not hungry. His face gaunt with worry as he entered the library and poured himself a large French brandy before he dropped wearily into a high-backed winged chair across the hearth from where his son sat. There was just one lamp lit on the far side of the book-lined room. Flames from the log fire splashed most of the library with constantly moving patterns of light and shade.

The elder Steele took a swallow of brandy and announced: 'Virginia's joined the Rebels, son.'

Adam merely nodded.

'Passed the secession ordinance today. April 17, 1861. It'll go down as the blackest day in the state's history.'

'You knew it would happen, Pa.'

'But hoped it wouldn't. I have some hopes in other directions, too.'

His son ignored the implied question to ask one of his own. 'What else did you find out?'

'President Lincoln has called a special session of Congress for July 4. Until then he intends to run the government more or less alone. And he's called for seventy-five thousand men to volunteer for ninety-day terms in the Union army. He'll need more than that for longer than that.

'Rumour is that Robert E. Lee is thinking of turning down a field command he's been offered and resigning the Union army. Doubtless to join the Confederacy.'

'He's a native-born Virginian.'

'So am I!' Ben Steele countered, anger putting sharpness in his tone.

'Me, too.'

Perhaps both men were surprised at the reversal of their usual roles – the younger Steele calm in face of the elder's display of temper. The father paused to regain his composure, then leaned forward in his chair, expression earnest in the flickering firelight.

'But we're all Americans, Adam. The new President has the capability of becoming a great man, given the opportunity. And this country can become even greater than it is. If it remains whole. And it can remain whole, son. If Jefferson Davis and his power-hungry bunch fail to win sufficient support. The traitors could be crushed. Just like that.'

He clicked thumb and finger.

'You're the traitor, Pa,' Adam Steele accused evenly. 'America's too big, which is why states were formed to govern themselves – '

'I don't need lessons in politics from you, boy!' Ben Steele snapped. 'And I resent being called a traitor by the son I fathered and raised!'

Adam sighed and pushed himself up from the chair, wincing at the pain the movement caused him. 'I'm sorry, Pa,' he said, expressing a genuine feeling. 'But my mind's made up and my horse is ready saddled in the stable. I'd have bedded him down again if there was no word about Virginia seceding.'

The soft-spoken words bit deep enough into Ben Steele to hurt him badly. And because he thought he saw a threat of tears in his father's eyes, Adam looked away from the anguished face.

'It's that kind of insular thinking that has caused this war,' the elder man said. 'Selfish thinking. People putting their own greed before the common good of all.'

The son started towards the door. 'I'm not greedy, Pa. I've always had more than I need. And want.'

'I know, son,' the father said with a crack in his voice and his face looking drawn with the effort of controlling the conflicting emotions he felt towards Adam. 'And I was able to provide that for you because of what Virginia gave me.'

His son continued on towards the door of the dimly lit room, back firmly turned against the pleading look which showed fleetingly in Ben's eyes. And the older man's temper, inherited by Adam, made an infrequent break through the usually calm and controlled surface.

'So go and join those other no-good hotheads who reckon Davis is the next best thing to the Son of God!' he snarled. 'But if you come out of it alive, don't ever return to this house!'

Adam halted with his hand on the door, which was half open. Rigid with emotion and unable to turn even his head to look back at his father in this uncharacteristic rage.

'You called me a traitor, boy! And that's something I'll never forget or forgive! It doesn't matter that you're my son! What galls me is that I heard it from the lips of somebody who's going to take up arms against the elected Government of the country of his birth! It's you and your kind who are starting this civil war, boy! You're the rebels and the traitors! Going

54

to fight for some cause dreamed up by a bunch of power-hungry fanatics!

'But it's a lost cause. Even before the first shots were fired, it was lost.' He had moderated his tone now, as he made a final attempt to win back his son with cold facts and reasoned logic. 'The Confederacy does not have a chance of winning, Adam. War has a high price, in human lives, raw materials and the products which are made from the materials to be used by the fighting men. Virginia, the Carolinas, Florida, Texas and the rest . . . Think of it, Adam. Cotton, tobacco, and men with twisted ideals. Against the industrialised northern states. Why, even if every man of fighting age in the south rallied to Davis, he couldn't arm you or supply you or take proper care of you if you were wounded.'

'Goodbye, Pa,' the younger Steele said as his father paused – perhaps for breath or maybe to marshal his thoughts to strengthen his argument.

'Adam!' Ben Steele cried. And his name, reaching him through the door he had closed behind him, sounded in Adam Steele's ears like a pathetically helpless plea voiced by a defeated man.

A doorway under the ornate staircase at the rear of the big hallway closed and Adam knew that at least one member of the household staff had overheard the low-keyed climax to the father and son quarrel.

Already fully dressed except for hat and topcoat, he looked neither to left nor right as he crossed the highly polished floor towards the double front doors of the big house, taking the missing items of clothing from the stand as he passed. But he did not halt to put them on until he was outside, under the shelter of the porch roof at the head of the steps.

Rain was falling steadily but not heavily from a low sky which concealed the moon and stars. The drops cooled the burning flesh of his cheeks as he stepped out from under the porch roof, hearing footfalls and the movement of a horse across gravel against the hiss of the rain. In the light from a few house windows, he saw the massively built Elroy leading the animal from the stable area.

'Bad news always travels fastest, Mr Adam,' the Negro said sadly. 'And I hears it's also said that folks that listens to what they shouldn't never hear good things.'

'Grateful to you, Elroy,' Adam said tautly as he accepted the reins of the big grey which was his favourite hunter. He swung up into the saddle and slid his booted feet into the stirrups before he added: 'Want you and your people to know something, feller.'

'What's that, Mr Adam?'

'That I'm not going away to fight so that your kind stay slaves.'

'I got no need to tell them that.'

Steele was unable to tell if the droplets of water coursing across the upturned face of the big black man were all spilled from out of the sky. He just nodded in acknowledgement.

'Mr Ben'll change his mind, Mr Adam. I bet he already has, deep down. Whatever happens, you'll be welcome back here.'

Steele turned his gravel-scarred face and cracked his eyes against the rain as he looked up at the big, rich house that had been his much-loved home for so long. And a lump rose into his throat. It took him several troubled seconds to swallow it before he could respond to Elroy in a normal tone. And he even managed to force a smile across his face as he said:

'Maybe, feller. But I reckon you'd have a better chance of that than me.'

'I'm sorry, Mr Adam, but I don't –'

Steele turned his gelding to head the animal down the driveway. And looked very youthful with the foolish grin still in place as he explained: 'You being the colour you are, Elroy. Every time you step into the house, you darken the doorstep.'

CHAPTER FOUR

KEYSVILLE was on the Danville and Richmond Railroad and it would have been easiest for Adam Steele to travel the seventy or so miles to the Virginia state capital by train. Because of the time of night he left home, it would have had to be a freight train. But even that would have been relatively comfortable compared to horseback riding through the dark and wet.

He considered the alternative only briefly as he passed through the quiet streets of the small town: and decided against it. For the train would be too quick in getting him to his destination. And he needed time to think. Not to reconsider his decision for his mind was firmly made up. Rather, to adjust to the new relationship with his father. They had disagreed before and on occasions the rifts between them had been deep and wide. Never so much as now, though. And never had the conflict erupted so abruptly. Nor had Ben Steele ever before shown so vividly that it was from him that Adam had drawn the seeds of violent temper. And it was this – this total lack of self-control displayed by his father – which gauged the enormous size of the breach which had been opened between them.

His father who had loved him from the moment of his birth had in a few moments come to hate him.

This, as he rode through the rain-swept night, Adam Steele came to accept. He was as much of a man as his father now and in truth it was a relief to have an opportunity to assert his individuality in such an uncompromising way.

Then he gave scant consideration to the basic rights and wrongs of their differences and rejected this line of thought because he had spent most of the day in reflection on this: and had decided to go with Virginia.

Thus, what concerned his conscience most during the long,

slow ride was whether or not he could respect his father's decision. Which was not to be a neutral in the just-started war. That was certain. Ben Steele was going to give active support to the northern states and was not about to reverse his position because his son had chosen to fight for the south.

So they were enemies and surely a soldier fought best if he hated his enemy.

Adam Steele grunted and the gelding pricked up his ears, as if expecting to receive a command from his rider. But no order came.

As the rider in the night acknowledged to himself that by accepting that his father hated him, he could generate the same feeling. By the not-so-simple process of burying the past in some dark and deep recess of his mind. So Benjamin P. Steele – no longer thought of as a father – was a hated enemy. But could he be respected for holding the views which made him such?

This was going to be far more difficult to decide. And as dawn broke under a slate-grey sky that continued to drop rain on to the lush greenness of Virginia, the weary and shivering Adam Steele was still host to doubts.

Unaware that as the son of an over-indulgent father, this was the first time in his life when he had asked for something and not been given it. And thus was resentment towards Ben Steele a colouring agent in every line of thought he sought to explore.

He rode into Richmond at mid-morning, his face gaunt from lack of sleep and his body aching and chilled by the long ride through the constant rain. He was not alone in being in the city in such a condition for the streets were crowded with others who had converged on Richmond with the same intention as himself. And many of them had come further and faster than him: others from not so far but on foot.

But, as he rode along 14th Street after crossing the James River and turned on to Cary, heading for the Capitol, he and the other exhausted travellers were lifted by the atmosphere of frenzied excitement which gripped the city.

Bells were ringing and almost every building was decked with flags. Many citizens of Richmond were attired in their finest clothes and many were drunk – these urging others to get into a like condition by thrusting bottles towards strangers who more often than not accepted the offered liquor. There was laughter and loud talk everywhere and for a moment

Steele reflected that a total stranger, newly arrived and unfamiliar with the current political situation, might on first impression think that a victory was being celebrated.

Then again, he extended his thoughts, perhaps that was just what was happening. For years there had been talk of the southern states separating themselves from the north. And now there was to be action, forced by men whose patience had run out and who realised that such a wrench could not be made bloodlessly.

Just for awhile as he rode the thronging, noisy streets, Steele felt himself a part of the excited scene. Grinning at the men and women who greeted him as a hero, taking swigs from the occasional uncapped bottle handed to him and bending down to accept kisses from the best-looking girls who gave them so willingly. But then, in quick succession, he saw a sour-faced old-timer who looked like an image of his father in defeated years to come and was kissed by a girl who shouted at him: 'My name's Diana, honey! Kill some Yankees for me!'

And it was thoughts of Diana Summers who only hours ago he had asked to marry him that abruptly set him apart from the festive scene. At no time during the long previous day or on the uncomfortable ride from Keysville to Richmond had he even considered her.

He was on Governor Street by then, heading like everyone else towards Capitol Square. The rain had stopped and the dull colour of the sky was showing signs of brightening on every horizon. Abruptly, the foolish grin slipping from his features, he jerked on the reins to turn on to a side street. His body feeling weak and used up again, as his mind was assaulted by fresh doubts.

The street was narrow, flanked by mean looking, dingy frame buildings. A sign caught his eye – ROOM AND BOARD. 25 CENTS. There was a hitching rail outside the grocery store next to the rooming house and he was just tying the gelding to this when a thin, grey-haired, middle-aged woman stepped from the open doorway under the sign.

'Reckon it ain't the store you want, young man,' she said, her voice sounding as weary as her face and bearing looked.

He glanced at the shuttered store and touched the brim of his Stetson. 'Looks closed, ma'am.'

'It is what it looks. On account that my husband that ran it has gone north.' There was suddenly pain mixed in with her misery. 'Kinda hopin' you wanted a room.'

'It no longer has to be hope, ma'am.'

'Call me Mrs Grady.' She turned her head to shout back into the house: 'John, come on out here. A horse to be took care of.'

A black youngster of about thirteen appeared from behind Mrs Grady and was tentative in his approach to Steele.

'Best you let John take the animal to the livery over on East Franklin,' the woman advised. 'Been lots of drinkin' all night and it's still goin' on. Drinkin' and mischief go hand in hand. And that's a fine-lookin' animal.'

Steele acknowledged her words with a nod and handed the gelding's reins to the boy: 'Grateful to you, son.'

Now knowing that this was a white man to be trusted, John grinned. 'Bring your tack right on back to this place, sir.'

'You hungry?' Mrs Grady asked as the horse was led away and she ushered her customer into the house.

'Reckon I will be when I get over being so tired. A place to sleep is what I need right now.'

'Up the stairs,' she instructed, waving towards the uncarpeted narrow staircase that angled up from the damp-smelling, ill-furnished hallway. 'An up-town hotel this ain't, young man. But you get clean linen and peace and quiet. Providin' none of that craziness happenin' elsewhere comes down here.' She continued on along the hallway and then called: 'Oh, take any room! We're empty!'

Steele opened the first door he came to on the landing and stepped into a ten-by-ten room furnished with just a bed and a bureau. One window which looked out through an old net curtain on the street. There was a pitcher of water in a basin on the bureau and when he had stripped down to his longjohns he washed and dried his hands and face.

While he was doing this, he thought of Diana and his father, Elroy, Jim Bishop and the plantation. Nothing specific about any of them. He merely thought about them. Then he got under the bedcovers and had no time to think of anybody or anything. Because he went immediately to sleep.

The room was not quite in darkness when he awoke, for a lamp which had been placed on the bureau was lit, the wick turned low so that just a glimmer of light spread from the glass funnel to enable him to see his surroundings. And seeing them he was able to recollect where he was and why he had come here.

In addition to the lamp which showed he had been visited in the room while asleep, the drape curtain was drawn across the window. And all his top clothes were gone from where he had discarded them untidily on the floor.

As he sat up in the bed and swung his feet to the floor, his belly rumbled its emptiness. And he smelled the aroma of simmering meat: realised that this was what had probably roused him. But he had slept long enough anyway and felt rested, warm and content.

A floorboard creaked under his weight and at once knuckles rapped on the door.

'You about, sir?' the Negro boy called.

'Sure am. But I can't come out for that good-smelling food until I get my clothes back.'

'You decent?'

'Reckon so.'

The door swung open and John entered, Steele's clothing draped neatly over each arm and wearing the Stetson at a jaunty angle on his head.

'They was all wet and muddy, sir. Mrs Grady had me fetch them and dry them and press them. She and me hopes you don't mind, sir.'

'Reckon I can afford that,' Steele told him, taking the clothing.

'Ain't no charge, sir. She and me are happy to be of service to a gentleman like yourself.'

He went out of the room, but only for a couple of seconds. Then re-entered, toting the gear taken from the back of the gelding.

'Told to tell you supper's ready whenever you are, sir.'

'What time is it?'

'Comin' up ten, sir. You just about slept the clock round.'

He went out and Steele washed up again, then shaved: using a mirror he found in a bureau drawer. The rooming house was as quiet as the woman had promised and if the celebrations were still taking place in the city, they had not spilled into this area.

Hunger proved a better barrier against bitter thoughts than had exhaustion and Steele's mind remained free of anything except the prospect of eating good food while he readied himself for the meal.

Then he followed the aroma down the unlit staircase and

was barred from entering the kitchen by the grinning John. Who swung open another door to usher him into the dining room.

'He's ready, Mrs Grady!' the boy yelled from where he held a chair for Steele at the big table that took up most of the floor space and was set for just one diner.

A table covered with a fine lace cloth. With, in front of where Steele sat, silver cutlery and condiment set and a side plate of high-quality porcelain, slightly chipped.

'It's plain food, sir,' the thin, grey-haired woman said as she set down a plate of beef stew in front of him and a heap of fresh-baked bread slices close by, while John spread a silk napkin across his lap. 'But I'm a good cook and there's plenty more if you need it. Just ring this if you do. Or when you're finished.'

John set down a small silver bell beside the plate of bread.

'Grateful to you, ma'am. Why don't you stay, though?'

'Us, sir?' the woman answered, surprised, when she saw that Steele had looked at both her and the boy as he made the invitation.

Her guest had already started eating and had to swallow a mouthful of the obviously long-time cooked, delicious tasting stew before he could reply. And waved a fork around the nine unoccupied chairs at the table.

'Room enough, I reckon.'

'You're a gentleman in every way, sir,' Mrs Grady said as she accepted the invitation and gestured with her head that the again tentative Negro boy should do the same.

Steele saw that she and John had scrubbed faces and were wearing what had to be their best clothes as he replied: 'And you give very good value for money, ma'am.'

'It ain't usual, sir,' John said, and hung his head under a withering look from the woman.

Steele grinned. 'Guessed it wasn't.'

Mrs Grady sighed. 'You ain't our usual kind of guest, sir. Knew that soon as you showed up. Polite and soft spoken. To me and the boy both. Tried to show my appreciation of that by having your wet things took care of. Saw from them – without being nosy, sir – that you been used to a whole lot better than this. So just doin' our best to make you comfortable.'

'Grateful to you.'

She waved a hand over the table and place setting. 'Long

way from the best, but it's the best I got.' Another sigh. 'Charlie and me never did make enough money for the best, and it wouldn't have been appreciated by our usual run of guests anyway.'

'Charlie's your husband?'

A nod. 'That's right, sir. He run the store next door durin' the day and give me a hand with this place early mornin's and nights. It was a good livin'. Nothin' fancy, but we got by well enough. Till the fightin' got to startin'. Charlie, he's from Boston. Same as me after I got here from Ireland. Native born, Charlie is. Said he just had to go north and volunteer for ninety days like Mr Lincoln has asked for.'

'And you, ma'am?'

'Spent twenty years buildin' up our two establishments, sir. Had to stay and take care of them. Hope this trouble ends soon. And if it don't, hope it doesn't come to Richmond. Mostly hope it ends soon, so Charlie don't have to risk bein' hurt.'

'Mr Grady, he's a good man,' John put in, his tone of enthusiastic admiration a counterpoint to the woman's dull-spoken words and sad expression.

'That he is,' she agreed. 'Who's doin' what he thinks is the right thing. Even though it'll likely cost him his life's work if it don't cost him his life.'

Steele was eating and posed the question with his coal-black eyes.

'Folks around here know where Charlie's gone and why he's gone, sir. We was filled up yesterday mornin' and empty within an hour of him leavin'. And I've heard talk in the neighbour-hood. Even if the troubles ended tonight, Charlie wouldn't be welcome when he came back. Civil War is a terrible thing, sir.'

'Reckon it is, ma'am,' Steele replied, matching her tone.

'You come to Richmond to join with the army, sir?' John asked.

'Ain't none of your business, boy!' the woman snapped at him.

'That's why I'm here,' Steele supplied.

Mrs Grady shook her head and sighed again. 'All good men have to do what they think is right, sir. But it's a tragedy. Why, God forbid, you and my Charlie could meet up on the same battlefield. And it would be each of your duties to try to kill each other. Each of you thinkin' you're doin' the right thing.'

'A damn shame,' John said.

'Don't swear at table,' Mrs Grady chided, lacking fervour. Then, after watching Steele mop up the final drains of gravy with a hunk of bread, asked: 'You want some more, sir?'

'No, ma'am. What I need now is something worthy of following such a fine supper.' He had to make an effort at heartiness while his mind was still reflecting on the subject of the conversation just ended, which had broadened his horizons: extended them beyond the selfish limits of sole concern with his father and himself.

'We don't serve liquor here, sir. But never has been any objection to guests bringin' in their own bottles. John'll go out and get you a –'

'Need to get a little air,' Steele interrupted. 'Be glad if you'll excuse me.'

Both the woman and the Nego boy looked suddenly nervous. She was the quicker at regaining her composure. 'Certainly, sir. But I'll need to lock the door behind you. Some of the talk I been hearin' has been real ugly. But you stay out long as you like. Always been a light sleeper. Last night didn't sleep hardly at all. Maybe not tonight, either. You just knock on the door when you come back, sir. And I'll hear you.'

Steele felt a rising resentment towards the woman as she spoke. Not because of her obvious fears of retaliation against herself for her husband's decision to support the north. Instead, for the clumsiness of her attempt to win his sympathy and through this his protection. Which might indicate that everything she had done for him was with the same aim in mind.

'I'll do that, ma'am,' he said quickly, rose from the table and went out into the hallway and then on to the street.

Bolts slid home to secure the door at his back and as he heard the sounds he regretted his abrupt departure. Realised that at least he could have offered a few words of reassurance to the woman and boy. Words that would have been devoid of any promise, but shown a considerate understanding of Mrs Grady's situation.

Then he growled: 'Shit, I owed Pa more,' as he moved hurriedly along the street towards the intersection with Governor, turning up his coat collar around his neck.

It was after eleven now and Richmond was relatively quiet: at least on its streets. The sky above was clear, the moon and stars bright, and a chill wind was blowing from the north-east, causing the many flags to flap noisily. And it was not long before Steele regretted not having gone upstairs to fetch his hat and topcoat before leaving Mrs Grady's rooming house.

But he walked fast to keep warm and in fifteen minutes found himself drawn by raucous sound to the façade of a riverside bar at the end of South 11th Street. And on the other side of the doorway and the steamed-up windows, under a garishly painted sign naming the place as Cassidy's, there was a promise of more warmth in abundance. Generated by the throng of customers crowded into the combination dance-hall and concert saloon. For several seconds, he stood at the doorway, gazing with something close to awe at a scene he had never before witnessed.

Cassidy's was an enormous cavern of a place. With gilt-framed mirrors hung along the two longest walls. On the right was a polished wooden bar running from the front to the rear of the place and to the left a double row of chair-ringed tables. At the far end from where Steele stood was a stage under a proscenium arch. The room was lit by two clusters of lamps hung chandelier fashion from the high ceiling.

A fiddler and a piano player were providing music on the stage, competing to be heard above the stamping feet of couples on the central dance area, the constant clink of bottles and glasses and the shouting and laughter of customers aligned along the bar or sprawled at the tables.

There were at least a hundred and fifty people in Cassidy's and a large proportion of them were drunk: getting drunker by the moment as they gulped at the liquor and beer served by a half-dozen barkeepers and twice as many girls who waited at table.

Tobacco smoke, liquor, perfume and sweat contributed to an atmosphere that, after breathing the clear, cold night air outside threatened to bring up from Steele's stomach the hardly yet digested meal he had eaten a few minutes earlier.

'Evenin', stranger. You wanna buy a lady a drink and then maybe dance with her?'

The girl in the low-cut red dress had to shout at Steele to make herself heard, pushing her face close to his as she gripped his arm. With dyed blonde hair and too much make-up on a badly blemished face she would have been unattractive at any time. With her big mouth wide to yell at him through a professional smile, sweat beads sheening her face and stale odours

5 65

erupting from her overblown body, Steele found her little short of revolting.

He used a hand to remove hers from his arm and yelled: 'Grateful to you, but maybe later. Looking for somebody.'

'Suit yourself,' the girl replied, and Steele thought he detected relief behind the weariness in her face as she abandoned the smile and swung around to rejoin a line of eight other dance-hall girls seated on a long bench to the left of the doorway.

The threat of nausea had passed now and Steele advanced on the bar, looking more closely at the clientele of Cassidy's. There were a lot more girls like those on the bench who had found customers more co-operative than Steele. And many more who had obviously been escorted to the place. The men were a mixture from several levels of society and of several races. A lot of them were seamen. Some had the look of river-side roustabouts. A few were as well dressed as Steele. And there was a group of a dozen soldiers in the company of four dance-hall girls spread around three tables.

The barkeeps, waitresses and hostesses all showed varying degrees of weariness after a long day. While those customers who were not slumped across tables in drunken stupors were obviously eager that this night should never end.

As he sought a gap among the drinkers at the bar, Steele overheard snatches of talk that revealed the drinking, dancing and laughter was a continuation of the revels he had seen when he rode into Richmond that morning. For almost all the talk was of war and of how the Confederacy would win the day at the expense of Yankee pride and Yankee lives.

'What can I get you?' a fat and sweating barkeep in a leather apron growled.

'Brandy. French.'

'It's the only kind we sell, mister.'

He reached for an unlabelled bottle off the shelf behind him and filled a shot glass brim-full. Steele paid for the drink and his grimace at the selection of the glass expanded after he had sipped the fiery liquor. The most that could be said for it, he thought, was that its pungent aroma acted to mask out many of the more unpleasant smells in Cassidy's.

'New in town, are you, young man?'

'I've been here before,' he answered as he turned to look at his questioner. Who was an army major in walking-out uniform, hatless and with his tunic unbuttoned. A man of about fifty with short-cropped black hair and a face tanned and roughened from long years of outdoor assignments. Only a slight reddening of his cheeks revealed that he had been drinking heavily.

'Not this part, I'd say.' He had the kind of voice that was easy to hear amid the din, although he did not seem to be shouting.

'No, sir. Whenever my father and I had business in town, we stayed up on Franklin Street.'

A nod. 'Fine hotels with fine bars serving the finest liquors.'

The major was drinking beer, which he finished and then banged the empty glass down on the bartop. Shouted: 'Give me another!' Then moderated his tone to say to Steele: 'You're not here on business now?'

'No, sir.'

'Came here like so many more to answer the call of Mr Jefferson Davis?'

He showed how he got such quick service by thrusting a half dollar at the bartender and telling him to keep the change.

'It's what I intended when I arrived this morning.'

The major narrowed his pale blue eyes. 'Changed your mind?'

'Giving it more thought, that's all.'

A wave of the hand to encompass their surroundings. 'Not the right atmosphere in which a man thinks at his best, I'd say.'

Steele set his hardly touched drink on the bar. 'It's new to me, sir. Like the rooming house I'm staying in. Need to get used to being in new places and doing new things if I join the army. Have freedom of choice now. Be different soon, I reckon.'

The major finished half his fresh drink at a swallow. Then shook his head. 'Haven't known you but a minute, young man. But I'd say you'll do all right. Just the kind of material we're looking for. Army needs men who do their own thinking. Don't act on impulse. Men of breeding and education. Little bit afraid, I'd say. Not of getting shot to hell by the Yankees. Of staying alive and handling the new style that's coming to you. That's good. Soldier that doesn't have some fear in him is no good to the army. Sure to get himself killed at the first opportunity and likely as not others as well.'

'Ask you a question, sir?'

'Surely.'

'What are you doing in this place?'

The major grinned. 'Besides getting drunk, you mean?'

'Seems most people are doing that.'

The uniformed man nodded. 'That's right, young man. And there are different kinds of drunken men. Happy ones and mean ones and in-betweens. I wouldn't choose to drink in an establishment like this. But my men heard about Cassidy's and reckoned to give it a try.' He jerked a thumb towards the three tables where other soldiers from privates to sergeants were sharing the company of a quartet of hostesses on the far side of the room. 'We're newly in from the Indian Territory. Recalled east by a friend of mine who knew it was my wish soon as a real war got underway. Men need to cut loose a little after near two years riding herd on hostiles in the middle of nowhere. After surviving that, hate to have any of them hurt in a bar-room brawl. Maybe worse than hurt on account of nobody can be trusted and maybe ninety per cent of the people in here are Yankee sympathisers.'

'Maybe I am, sir.'

'Maybe you are,' the major allowed. 'All you got to do is something to prove it. And I'll kill you. Hope you're not, though.'

His tone and attitude remained matter-of-fact. But just for a moment, in his pale blue eyes, there was a dangerous glint: and while it showed, he looked not at all drunk. Then he laughed. Deeply, so that his belly moved.

'But I'm not often wrong in my judgement of men. And I'd say you're for the Confederacy. That you'll volunteer and do your damnedest to win victory for us.'

'Adam! Adam! Adam Steele!'

The shouting of his name from over near the doorway prevented Steele from replying immediately to the major. Who realised that this was the man being called and turned to locate the shouter. It was the fat Nick Kane, who was in company with Banning, Davidson, Shotter, Harding and Cliff Gordon. All of them obviously drunk as they staggered through the dancing couples towards the centre of the bar where Steele stood. And all of them save the temporarily disfigured Gordon grinning their pleasure at seeing Steele.

'You'll excuse me,' the major growled, blatantly disapproving either of the interruption or the group of young men responsible for it. 'I'll leave you with your friends.'

He moved away, to find a space further along the bar where he could catch the attention of a tender and order another beer. As Steele was surrounded by the group from Keysville, all but Gordon slapping his back, pumping his hand, laughing and yelling their delight that he had come to Richmond. From the babble of voices, Steele was able to learn that they were all now in the Confederate States Army and were to report to training camp the next morning. And it was their intention on this last night as civilians to tour every bar in the city.

For his part, Cliff Gordon turned his back on the happy reunion scene, bellying up to the bar and demanding a whiskey.

'How long you been in town?'

'You in the army yet?'

'Have a drink, old buddy!'

'Where you staying?'

'Who's the major?'

The questions came fast, shouted louder than necessary by the liquored-up young men. By Banning, Davidson, Harding and Kane as Conrad Shotter got between Steele and the bar to order a round of beer. Genuinely pleased to see the people from Keysville, Steele began by answering the first few questions: but his responses were lost under more shouted queries. Then interest in specifics was lost as a half-dozen dance-hall girls advanced on the group, bodies swaying and professional smiles pasted to their faces. So he just grinned and drank the beer Shotter thrust at him, listening to the naïve banter of the country boys and admiring the way in which the hard-bitten city women almost concealed their boredom as they pretended to enter into the spirit of things. He stood on the sidelines without arrogance, aware that had he been as drunk as his friends he would have shown himself to be as much a country bumpkin as they.

The women were angling for drinks while a sweating and eager bartender waited with ill-concealed impatience, ignoring demands from unaccompanied men. One of whom was Cliff Gordon, having knocked back a whiskey at a single swallow.

'Dance first!' the squint-eyed Shotter demanded.

'Damn right!' Andy Harding added, not at all like his usual quiet self.

'Haven't had a woman in my arms for at least three hours!' Brew Davidson yelled, sweat beads running out of his bright ginger hair and streaming down his flushed face.

'Custom of the house!' the bartender snarled, suddenly grim-faced. 'No one gets to dance with a Cassidy's girl until they bought her a drink!'

'Who says?' the obese Nick Kane countered in the same tone. As the attention of everyone within earshot was directed at this area of the bar.

'Cassidy!' the bartender growled, stabbing a thumb at the centre of his broad chest. 'And that's me, fatso!'

With Gordon having detached himself from the group, Kane had apparently elected himself spokesman and leader of the young men from Keysville. More drunk than Steele had ever seen him, the small town reporter spread a scowl across his fleshy features and lifted his shoulders. As, along the bar, the other tenders sensed the threat of trouble and curtailed serving customers.

'Give the ladies what they drink, feller,' Steele said before Kane could voice a retort to Cassidy.

Cassidy gave a curt nod and reached under the bartop to produce another unlabelled bottle. Then, as he set down five glasses beside it, he growled: 'Red wine imported from France. Dollar a shot.'

'You didn't have to –' Kane started.

'And another round of beer,' Steele cut in. 'Whiskey for that feller.'

He waved a hand towards Cliff Gordon.

'I'll take it, Steele,' the man with the badly marked-up face called. 'But all you're buyin' is the liquor. There's some trouble Steele dollars can't smooth over.'

The implication of Gordon's words made the threat a purely personal one. Which was of no interest to anyone else who heard them: as the dance-hall girls, high-priced drinks in their hands, broke into fast talk and shrill laughter to dispel the final shreds of disgruntlement caused by the house rule. Which they did easily, setting the seal on their success when they urged the young men out on to the dance-floor.

The now impassive-faced Cassidy shifted his hard eyes between Steele and Gordon as he poured liquor into the latter's shot glass. 'I ain't gonna thank you, dude,' he growled. 'We can handle our own trouble if needs be. But best when the customers take care of their own business. So if you and him want to mark each other up some more, advise you to do it outside these premises.'

Gordon scowled and hunched his shoulders, facing the bar, elbows on it. Steele gave an almost imperceptible nod and turned his back on the bar to gaze at the dancers: as he did this caught a glimpse of the major who, in the part of a second their eyes met, displayed an approving smile.

'You found lots of somebodies, mister. So now it's maybe later?'

It was the dyed blonde in the red dress who had tried to interest Steele when he first entered Cassidy's. The smell of her body sweat was less pungent now, but her hard professionalism was still just as obvious. Beyond her, visible between the circling dancers and the drinkers at the bar, Steele could see the bench by the door which was now occupied only by a very fat, extravagantly dressed woman of sixty or so. Who used a fan to stir the smoke-layered air in front of her over-painted face as she watched for the outcome of this new attempt to win Steele's approval.

'The brandy here is likely to rot a man's guts, lady,' Steele said evenly. 'The beer is just about under the boil. And I wouldn't touch any of Cassidy's women with the prick of my worst enemy.'

She listened without a flicker of expression. But was suddenly anxious to be somewhere else and turned to hurry away when Cliff Gordon taunted:

'That's the Steeles for you. All money and no balls.'

Cassidy was close enough to hear the insult. Too far away to have overheard the opening for it. But he could see Steele and saw the way he became rigid for a moment before he started to turn.

Gordon was also turning, after pushing away from the bar. Not far enough away, though.

'Behind you, Cliff!' Steele yelled.

Gordon expressed scorn for what he considered a feeble attempt to distract him. This as the drinkers between and behind the two Keysville men followed the example of the dyed blonde and shuffled hurriedly back from the threat of trouble.

Probably there were clubs positioned at intervals along the whole length of the bar. Certainly there was one immediately to hand for Cassidy, who snatched it out from under the bartop, leaned forward and swung it in a short but powerful arc.

'Cliff!' the bespectacled Cornell Banning roared from the centre of the dance-floor as he glimpsed what was happening.

If Gordon heard his name, there was not even a split second in which he could consider the reason it was shouted. For the short length of rounded timber cracked against the back of his

71

skull: his eyes rolled up in their sockets and the lids snapped together as he pitched to the beer-and-spittle-run floor.

'Get him outta here!' Cassidy roared.

Here and there throughout the big room, interest had been captured by events at the centre of the long bar. But most of those who witnessed what happened immediately returned to what had occupied them previously: convinced that the experienced Cassidy had once more skilfully averted serious trouble in his place. Even those in the immediate area of the clubbing made to return to their positions at the bar: assuming Steele was advancing to do as Cassidy had ordered.

But Steele stepped over the unmoving form with the blood-matted hair. And reached out to fasten a double-handed grip on the shirt of Cassidy. Took hold of the fabric at each shoulder while the bigger man was still leaning across the bar to scowl down at the unconscious Gordon.

At first impression, because of his slight build and his choice of dudish clothes, Adam Steele did not look strong. But it was a mistaken impression, for his muscles had been developed to their limit by the long hours of hard manual labour he had engaged in alongside the Negroes back on the plantation. And it was anger rather than physical strain which formed his snarling expression as he jerked Cassidy off his feet and over the bar. He stepped backwards as he did this, unconcerned by the other man's bellowed curse and attempt to swing the club.

Then, as Cassidy's bootcaps scraped across the polished bar-top and his whole body weight was held by the double-handed grip on his shirt, Steele brought up his right knee. The length of travel was short, but it was fast and hard.

Steele grimaced as he felt the teeth in Cassidy's open mouth stab at his thigh. But pain was negated by a sense of triumph as he heard the man's curse curtailed by a crunch of bone and became aware of the warmth of his victim's blood on his leg. He released his hold and Cassidy crashed to the floor and lay still.

The sound of the fall competed only with the fiddle and piano music and a few loud-voiced conversations from far corners of the room. Then, a few moments later, silence descended over the entire cavern of a place as musicians and patrons alike became self-consciously aware that the noise they were making was surrounded by tense silence.

Total silence lasted no longer than a second. For somebody

rasped in awe: 'The dude laid out Cassidy!'

The fat woman sprang up from the bench and vented a shrill scream. Which triggered a cacophony of shouting, laughter and cheers. Even some hand-clapping.

Just one of the tenders had to move a couple of feet to the side to lay hands on a club. The other four had only to reach under the bartop immediately in front of where they stood. As, on the stage, the fiddler and the piano player reached under their seats to grasp similar lengths of timber before they got to their feet. While, at various points on and around the dance-floor, men who until now had acted like customers, abruptly made it known to those close by that they were in the business of quelling trouble in Cassidy's.

Two bartenders advanced on where Steele stood, swinging clubs in their right hands while their left hands trailed on the bartop: fastened a grip to power their leaps over the barrier as they closed with him.

Steele forced his temper under control as he looked to left and right – with no time to glance over his shoulder. Grinned at what he saw: the scene to either side of him speeding the process of putting behind him his anger at Cassidy. That had found an outlet. And now he could enjoy himself. For it seemed that a city bar-room was no different from the kind back home in at least one respect. When most of the customers were liquored up and somebody started a brawl, everybody joined in.

Abruptly, the noise level in the big room rose to ear-splitting levels as screaming women raced clear of trouble and men extended it. For the first few seconds it was customers against the men who tried to defend Cassidy's. But there were not enough of the latter to provide opponents for everyone who felt the urge to hit somebody else.

So seamen of one nationality rounded on those from a different country. Army men lashed out at civilians. And here and there men who had been drinking convivially together began to trade punches.

Tables crashed over and bottles and glasses spilled to the floor and shattered – those that were not saved to be used, along with chairs, as weapons.

Steele heard what was happening but received only fleeting glimpses of the eruption around him. For he had to deal with the two aproned bartenders who leapt down at him, clubs whirling.

He chose to go towards his attackers rather than to retreat: snatching the advantage of surprise because the bartenders least expected him to do this.

He hit the one to his right in the throat with both hands clasped into a single fist, making the connection while the man was still in mid-air. Ducked instinctively and felt the slip-stream move his hair as the club of the second man missed his skull by part of an inch. Whirled and had time to grasp an ankle of this man. Held it high so that his new victim could get only one foot to the floor. Not enough for the man to achieve balance when he landed. Pushed the leg away from him, and launched a right cross that hit the side of a sweating face with a pleasing sound.

The first man to land badly was back on his feet by then. In a half-crouch, arm swinging back to arc the club towards the target again. But the wrist of his club hand was suddenly caught from behind. And he snapped his head around to curse at Cornell Banning whose triumph turned to fear when he saw the bartender's face. But then another right cross connected, Steele's fist catching the side of the jaw this time. The bartender was tough enough to take the blow and remain conscious: but it sent him to the side and his temple banged against the edge of the bartop. The skin split and runnels of blood trickled down the woodwork towards where its former host lay curled up and senseless.

'Grateful, feller,' Steele said, as he heard footfalls behind him and whirled.

'You're grateful?' Banning gasped after a fast swallow.

And followed Steele's example of ducking as a bearded man in the uniform of the British Royal Navy hurled a chair towards them. The chair sailed over both of them, across the bar and shattered a half-dozen bottles aligned on a shelf.

'Not the booze, you friggin' idiot!' a man shrieked. And was probably aware that the bottle he smashed over the sailor's head was empty.

The seaman merely shook his head, scattering shards of glass about him, turned on his assailant, picked up the screaming man bodily and hurled him over the bar. With the ease of an experienced hand tossing an underweight cotton bale.

The man's shriek was curtailed as he crashed into more bottles, breaking them and the mirror behind them before he bounced to the floor.

'Adam, I think we should get out of here!' Banning yelled, tugging at Steele's sleeve as the British seaman turned to face them again, massive fists clenched and looking more menacing than ever with blood from his cut scalp running down his face and into his beard.

'That's the way, boys!' the Britisher taunted. 'Run, just like all you poxy Southerners are gonna run from the Yankees!'

The man was even bigger and broader than Elroy and could probably have taken Steele and Banning with smooth ease. But his decrying of the south was heard by several other men who, whether fighting each other or not, abandoned what had been occupying them and rounded on the foreigner.

'Eat them words, you sonofabitch!' one man shrieked as he and a half-dozen others powered towards the seaman: and knocked him to the floor by force of number.

The attack was seen by another British naval rating, who summoned help from more of his kind by thrusting two fingers in his mouth and sounding a piercing whistle.

Thus were other man-to-man fights broken off as uniformed figures converged upon the heap of writhing men on the floor.

Steele wrenched free of Banning's grip and vaunted up on to the bartop: raked his eyes over the mêlée.

He saw the squint-eyed Conrad Shotter down on all fours, trying to get up, blood on his face. Andy Harding and Nick Kane trading punchings in orthodox boxing style with a couple of roustabouts. While the ginger-haired Brewster Davidson was using a chair to fend off a big army sergeant, much as a trainer might keep a wild animal at bay. He seemed to be protecting a pretty Oriental girl who was pressed to the wall behind him.

Elsewhere, personal and group fights were continuing, those involved either unaware of the major event at the centre of the bar, or choosing to ignore it. While behind the bar a half-dozen men were crouched on the floor, sucking free liquor from bottles. Blood stains were everywhere. So, too, were the senseless forms of men who had been beaten to the floor or were slumped across the bar and overturned tables. Most of the women were crowded into two groups at either end of the big room. Those who did not work in the place looked scared. While the dance-hall girls appeared to be enjoying this break from routine, ignoring the screaming fat woman who was apparently their boss.

Steele snapped his head around as he heard a noise behind

him. And saw the major in process of getting to his feet from where he had been crouched in the cover of the bar.

'Man who goes to the aid of one of his own is fine material, young man,' the army officer said evenly as he buttoned up his tunic. 'That's especially so if he has no reason to like the man in trouble. Law'll be here, soon. Richmond gaols are no better than those any place else.'

Steele nodded in acknowledgement and leapt down to the floor. 'Get Cliff and take him out!' he yelled at Banning, pointing to a doorway beside the proscenium arch at the back of Cassidy's. 'Be right with you.'

He went to get Shotter first, who had made it to his feet. And was in danger of being knocked down again by an army private who had just finished off a city-suited man. Steele sent the army man into a staggering run by thudding a shoulder into his back. Then caught hold of Shotter's arm and jerked him into movement.

'Terrific, old buddy,' the groggy Shotter growled as he focused his squinting eyes on Steele. 'Let's go get them women now!'

Andy Harding had floored his opponent and was trying to drag the second roustabout off the fat Nick Kane who was down on his back. Steele gave him a hand and the surprised man suddenly found himself slithering across the floor on his rear end.

'I could've beat the bastard!' Kane blurted, and a piece of broken tooth shot out with the final word.

'Sergeant!' Steele yelled at the non-com who was still trying to get by Davidson and the chair to reach the terrified Chinese girl.

The man whirled, fists clenched.

'The major's ready to leave!' Steele snapped. 'Law's been called.'

Just for a moment, the scar-faced sergeant seemed not to have heard the words: looked ready to lunge at Steele. But something caught his eye and he looked away – saw a signal from the major.

'Shit,' he muttered, with a glance at the girl. 'I don't believe it's true. Who needs to look, anyway?'

'What at?' Brew Davidson asked, tossing away the chair.

'That her kind's east to west instead of north to south,' the sergeant called after him as he lunged away, to collect up the army men much as Steele had brought the Keysville group together. 'I don't wanna look.'

'I come with you, please!' the Chinese girl, who was no more than fourteen, pleaded.

Davidson took her wrist and jerked her after him as he followed the others. Heading for the closed door where Cornell Banning was rested, breathless with the effort of dragging the heavy Gordon out of the centre of the fighting.

'Door's locked!' the bespectacled man groaned.

It was Harding who kicked at the lock and the door swung away from them. 'Not now,' he announced.

Steele helped Banning with the unconscious man and led the way along a passage with steps to the stage on one side and doors on the other. Kane pushed past them to smash open the door at the end that gave on to a yard with a gap in the fence on one side. The air smelled strongly of the James River and when they went through the gap they could see the moon-silvered water at one end and the start of South 11th Street at the other.

Banning released Cliff Gordon and rasped: 'That's far enough, Adam. We've done more than he deserves already.'

Steele heard a girlish squeal of delight and whirled to see that Shotter and Harding were holding the young whore's arms against the fence while Kane raised her skirts and Davidson fumbled with her underwear.

'See, you good to me, I be good to you!' the girl cried glee-fully. 'Special price. Fifty cents only each.'

'Far enough for me,' Adam Steele spat out, allowing Gordon's shoulders and head to bang down to the alley surface. 'Maybe I'll see you fellers around.'

He moved off along the alley, away from the river and towards the street.

'This I gotta see!' Andy Harding yelled.

'Yeah, if it's true, it has to be really something!' Nick Kane added excitedly.

'Just the usual will be all right with me,' Shotter announced.

Footfalls sounded in the alley behind Steele. Receding. As Banning went to join the others crowded in front of the young Chinese girl who was shaking with giggles as her lower body was stripped of clothing.

The stoutly built walls of Cassidy's dance-hall and concert saloon acted to subdue the sounds from within, but it was plain to hear that the fighting was continuing unabated. Even though the sergeant had performed his assignment and pulled the rest of the soldiers out of the fray. For all of them were now on the street, fumbling to smarten themselves up and wipe blood off their hands and faces under the authoritarian eye of the major.

'On enlistment duty right now, young man,' the major called to Steele as he moved along the opposite sidewalk. 'Camped out near the Tredegar Iron Works. If you've a mind, ask for me by name. Major Miles Vernon.'

Steele raised a hand and continued on along the street. Heard hoofbeats and the clatter of wheelrims: had to wait to cross over until three paddy wagons had raced by.

Just before he turned off Governor Street to round the corner and go towards Mrs Grady's rooming house, he smelled burning. Or rather, the ashes of a fire. For the flames had long been out and the street was quiet again after the city fire service had left the scene. Only the thin woman and the young Negro were still about: trying to find anything that was worth salvaging among the heap of grey ashes and charred timber that was all that remained of the rooming house and the store. Close to the woman and boy, Steele could smell scorched flesh where they had been too quick to handle uncooled pieces of the wreckage.

'Whatever you left in the room, sir, it's gone,' Mrs Grady said as she heard Steele's footfalls and peered towards him, the whites of her eyes showing up starkly against her sooted face.

He shook his head. 'It wasn't much, ma'am.'

'They said they only wanted to burn the store. Because it was Charlie's. But the flames spread.'

'Anything I can do?'

Because of her darkened face, he got his first clue to her anger from the way her skinny body stiffened. 'You can go to hell, mister! Same as every other man who wants to fight a war! Includin' Charlie! Kill each other and go to hell! So as decent folks can live peaceful and free of hate!'

Steele thought of his father, of Cliff Gordon, of Cassidy and a lot of faces without names who had been in the place at the end of South 11th Street. And muttered:

'No use telling me, ma'am. Best you pray to God. He's the only one can work miracles.'

CHAPTER FIVE

IT was July in western Virginia and the summer weather was fine, the mountainous country beautiful to look at. Adam Steele had worn the stiffness out of his uniform fabric but the polished buttons gleamed and the braid insignia of his rank as cavalry lieutenant still looked brand new.

He was no exception among the troop of fifty men he led out of Beverly that beautiful summer morning with orders to join the more than four thousand Confederate soldiers camped at nearby Rich Mountain. For during the few short weeks since he was commissioned as an officer, he had put into practice the theory that one of the strongest foundation stones upon which to build military discipline was the instilling into men of the need for smartness.

The man who had instructed him in this and many other aspects of soldiering was Major Miles Vernon, the veteran of active service in Indian Territory and with earlier experience of the Mexican War who Steele had first met before the brawl at Cassidy's dance-hall and concert saloon.

After leaving Mrs Grady and the Negro boy among the debris of the fire, Steele had got his horse from the livery stable and led him, saddleless, up town. Where he checked into the finest hotel which Richmond offered: to sleep in a sumptuously furnished suite and then breakfast in style. His decision to indulge in such luxury consciously influenced by the drinking and whoring spree of the other Keysville men who had come to Richmond. And after breakfast he had purchased a new saddle and ridden out to the army camp at the Tredegar Iron Works to accept the invitation of the major: content with how he had spent his final few hours as a civilian.

The tented enlistment centre was crowded with eager volunteers, many of them impatient with the harassed regular soldiers who were greatly understrength for processing the unexpectedly high number of men who had flocked to answer the call of Jefferson Davis.

Adam Steele, accustomed by what he considered his birthright to privileged treatment, felt no guilt at the line jumping which was involved when he mentioned Major Vernon's name to a contemptuous sergeant. And thus there was no reason to feel better when he discovered that he was not unique in this respect. For a score of other men from the same strata of Virginia society as himself had also been invited to bypass the normal induction routine. Either by Vernon, a colonel, another major or two captains who formed the officer selection board.

The interviews were short and designed to elicit from the men the degree of experience they had in riding, hunting, shooting and superintending the workers in the various businesses run by their families. Steele was to learn later from Vernon that the selection board had also tested the men for integrity – that much was known about the interviewees before they arrived at the camp. And that almost half were rejected as officer material because they embroidered their actual skills and experience.

Just one question asked of Steele gave him pause for thought: when the grey-moustached colonel said:

'I've met your father from time to time, son. Especially recently up in Washington during Abraham Lincoln's election campaign. Guess he's not too happy about you being here? How do you feel about that?'

Steele knew the answer he was to give. Reflected just for a few moments upon the scene he had witnessed the previous night as the white woman and the black boy sifted through what was left of their home.

'I think he's wrong, sir. And he must think I'm wrong. If there wasn't a division of opinion there wouldn't be any war. He could lose everything, just as I could. Just as everyone involved could. Anyone prepared to take such a risk deserves respect.'

'Obliged to you, son. Just wait outside for awhile, will you.'

A brief smile from Vernon told Steele he had handled himself well. But during the next few weeks there were few signs of approval from any quarter as he and the other men recommended for commissions underwent the same rapid training programme as other volunteers. On the contrary, there was resentment both from fellow trainees doomed to serve in the ranks of the CSA and from the instructors who were veteran regular army non-coms soured by the knowledge that they were teaching civilians destined to be giving orders to them shortly.

For the chosen few who realised their potential as officer material at ill-equipped camps around Richmond, the next phase of the training schedule had to be cut to the bone and was comprised mostly of lectures by Major Vernon and other experienced career soldiers on the strategies and tactics of attack and withdrawal in battle and skirmish situations.

Union strategy was the reason for the curtailment of training.

Aware that the western area of Virginia was sympathetic to the North and that a strong body of opinion favoured a break-away and the formation of a new state, Union forces were on the move. Yankee soldiers, under the command of Major General George B. McClellan were already marching along the Baltimore and Ohio Railroad tracks and had routed a small force of Rebels at Philippi. Now McClellan and his Ohio and Indiana men were pressing further east, their morale high after the small victory. And it was obvious the Union forces had designs on the town of Staunton which commanded the upper end of the Shenandoah Valley, and the equally important prize of Harper's Ferry.

Realising his vulnerability, Brigadier General Joseph E. Johnston had withdrawn his troops from Harper's Ferry as soon as the Union forces entered Virginia. But Robert S. Garnett, an officer of similar rank was holding out at Beverly which strad-dled the turnpike to Staunton. He needed reinforcements, though. And Adam Steele was one of the shavetail lieutenants assigned to head a troop of mostly raw volunteers into the high-wooded country of western Virginia.

They arrived at the small town late at night: and early next morning had to leave again. As did every other Rebel at the garrison, with orders to dig in at either Laurel Hill or Rich Mountain which were the two main passes through the mountains.

Steele's troop were assigned to join the smaller of the two defensive groups at Rich Mountain: smaller because Garnett considered it had better natural defences than Laurel Hill.

And certainly the pass looked to be an insurmountable obstacle to Steele and most of his men as they rode into it in columns of two. But Sergeant Dwight Jacobs, one of Vernon's men, who the young lieutenant had elected to be his second in command of the troop, evidently did not share Steele's enthusiasm.

Jacobs was a six-feet-tall, broadly built man of forty or so with a round face covered with burnished skin that looked to have the texture of well-used leather. Initially disgruntled to be assigned to the troop of a ninety-day volunteer officer, he had gradually mellowed in his attitude: flattered to be asked for advice and getting close to admiration for the lieutenant when this advice was heeded.

It was midday and very hot when the leading riders of the column were in a position to survey the Rich Mountain pass: where artillery pieces were already in position among the timber to either side of a log-built shack and infantrymen were busily digging trenches.

For a few moments, Steele smiled as his black eyes took in the sights and his ears picked up the sounds of steady, not hectic, activity. But even before he glanced to the side and saw the frowning profile of the veteran sergeant, his mood had begun to dissipate.

The rigours of training camp were distant memories, seldom recalled during the easy ride from Richmond to Beverly. During the night and early morning in Beverly there had been a very discernible atmosphere of tension as plans were made for a military withdrawal from the town. But out in the open, verdant country, Steele was again visited by a sense of well-being. And it was obvious his men felt the same way. They were clean in body and clothing and had full bellies. From briefings and rumours they all knew that they would soon be required to engage the enemy but not one of them had seen or heard a sign of the enemy's presence in the area – beyond the repercussions of this presence visibly at Beverly. And out in the clear, bright, quiet sunlit air of the Virginia mountains it was difficult to visualise the sights and sounds of war.

Until they came upon the scene of activity at the pass. When the first thought to enter men's heads was one of relief as they looked from the mass of defenders, to their fellow troopers and then down at their own uniformed frames. Men from diverse backgrounds, of all ages, sizes, shapes and characters who under normal circumstances might not give a thought one to the other. But in this abnormal circumstance they were as

82

one, with Confederate grey the visible sign of this bond.

Thus, it was comforting to see so many of their kind toiling to defend the pass and, it followed, to protect each other.

But from what?

This question which was posed from out of that dark recess of the mind which harboured the ability to be afraid, was what caused an icy sensation to ripple down the back of Steele. And doubtless affected many of the men riding behind him.

The euphoria of the war's opening was finished. The pitifully short training period was complete. The pleasant days of riding through unspoilt countryside had come to an end. Up here among the wooded peaks along the western ridges of the Alleghany Mountains on this July day, the preparations for war were already scarring the natural beauty of the area. For the ugly muzzles of six-pounder field guns protruded from thickets; heaps of freshly dug earth lay on the turf in front of deep trenches; several trees had been felled to provide fuel for the more than twenty cooking fires which were scattered throughout the pass; and lush vegetation had been trampled and wrenched out by the roots as the soldiers made their preparations – to take part in a shooting war.

'Something wrong, sergeant?' Steele asked, noting that the men they were reinforcing paid scant attention to the newly arrived column of clean and unsweating troopers.

'War's wrong, sir,' the leather-skinned non-com answered dully, shifting his jaundiced gaze to Steele for a moment. 'Unless it's against foreigners or Indians and I figure Indians are foreigners anyway. But if we gotta fight, we gotta fight. Just hope the colonel knows what he's doin'.'

Jacobs was referring to Colonel John Pegram, who was in command of the Rich Mountain force.

'You see anything to make you think he doesn't?' the lieutenant queried.

'No, sir. But I ain't never heard of him or what he's done before. And I ain't never fought in this kind of country. Nor fought any enemy except for hostile redskins. So I ain't in no position to criticise. Just thinkin' aloud is all. Since you asked.'

'None of us is in any position to criticise, sergeant,' Steele growled. Asserting his authority for the benefit of the men close enough in the column to have overheard the exchange. It was not the first time he had felt it necessary to do this for he had become aware early on that some of the troopers were scornful of the way he, an officer, relied so much on the veteran sergeant. 'And I just don't mean those in this troop. A lot of men on both sides are going to have to learn things the hard way.'

'And there ain't no better way to learn anythin' than by mistakes, sir,' Jacobs responded dully.

The head of the column had ridden through the first line of defence by then, and Steele held up a hand to call a halt, then executed a copybook salute as a tunic-less captain of infantry emerged from a large bell tent.

'Lieutenant Steele reporting with B Troop, sir,' he snapped. 'Orders to –'

The pale and fleshy faced captain responded to the salute with a hand brushing the peak of his forage cap. 'Sure, lieutenant. Good to have you along. Make your way to the rear and set up camp. There'll be a briefing session in the command quarters at four this afternoon. Word is the Yankees will be here before nightfall.'

Steele threw up another salute, which was ignored by the captain who swung away to hurry in the direction of a gun battery. Just for a moment, Steele met the hard-eyed stare of a private helping to stack shells beside one of the six-pounders. They were the resentful eyes of Cliff Gordon, staring out of a face which – like Steele's – had healed of scars caused by the gravel on the driveway of the plantation outside Keysville.

While his men made camp on an area of sloping ground behind a stand of timber, Steele climbed further up the incline to survey from a high vantage point the layout of the defensive positions and the terrain to the west over which the Union forces were expected to advance. And, to his mind, Colonel Pegram had done everything possible to secure the pass. He based this opinion on the lectures he had listened to during officer training and on his own judgement of what was sound commonsense.

But as he descended the slope towards the cavalry troop's encampment, he again experienced the icy chill down his back which he knew to be nothing else but sheer fear.

'Reckoned Steele pull would have bought you better than lieutenant's rank, *sir*.'

The big-built Cliff Gordon emphasised the courtesy title to make it sound like a sneer as he stepped from behind a boulder and a thicket of brush. But then he altered his expression to a contemptuous grin as he saw the startled look on Steele's face.

Steele fought against self-anger that he had allowed Cliff Gordon to see his obvious fear. And could think of no way to tell the Keysville man he was not afraid of him – without revealing the humiliating truth.

'No money was involved, *soldier*!' he answered, and added the emphasis simply to impress on the other man that he was now subject to army discipline.

'Maybe it didn't change hands, but it was involved sure enough.'

Steele pursed his lips, still having to make an effort to control and hide his anger which was now directed solely at Gordon.

'Anything you want, feller?' he said, managing to keep his tone even. 'Beyond letting me know yet again how much you hate my guts for being born rich?'

'Say thanks, *sir*,' he replied grudgingly with a sneer in the word still. 'I thought you was tryin' to sucker me in that saloon. I'm told I gotta thank you as well for gettin' me out of the place.'

'Forget it.'

'Now I've said thanks, I have.'

He spun around then, and went from sight between the boulder and the brush. And between the sound of two heavy footfalls, Steele heard him spit. Convinced Gordon had intended the spit to be heard, Steele opened his mouth to yell for the artillery man to come back. But smothered the impulse. Cliff Gordon was not under his immediate command and to bawl him out for failing to salute an officer and showing disrespect in other ways would achieve nothing with lasting effect.

So he continued on down to the camp, reflecting upon how the other men from the Keysville area had fared after their induction into the Confederate States Army.

At camp, he took a plate of lamb stew into his pup tent and ate alone. Then, after the eating utensils had been cleaned, he ordered a weapons inspection which produced no cause for complaint. As the inspection ended, a runner arrived from the command quarters: with instructions that Steele should draw up a duty roster which assigned six of his troop at a time to stand picket guard at the rear of the camp.

This done, the lieutenant withdrew to his tent again and checked over his own weapons.

His sabre could not be sharper nor shined brighter. His .36 calibre Navy Model Colt had an even sheen of light oil and was

85

fully loaded. And there was not a speck of dust in the smooth bore barrel of the .54 Sharps carbine.

'Time to get up to command, sir,' Sergeant Jacobs called after slapping a hand on the tent flap. 'Nearin' four o'clock.'

The reminder interrupted Steele's thoughts which had again turned to what might happen during the impending attack: such a futile dwelling on the unknown future triggered by his examination of the weapons. An inspection not unlike that he had made many times before – of other, better guns than these. In the late evening or the pre-dawn before he joined his father and friends of his father for a duck shoot or some other pleasurable gunsport over a far distant stretch of Virginia countryside.

'Grateful to you, sergeant,' he responded, jerking his mind back to the present as he slid the sabre into its scabbard and buttoned the holster flap over the revolver butt.

At the briefing, Adam Steele's initial estimation of Colonel John Pegram as a commanding officer went up. He also decided that he liked the handsome, neatly bearded colonel as a gentleman as well as an officer.

Pegram was pointed and concise in dealing with the business at hand. Intelligence had been received that McClellan planned to feign an attack on the large Confederate force at Laurel Hill: then switch his men towards Rich Mountain with the intention of surprising the Rebels dug in here. There would be no surprise now. An artillery barrage would be poured down at the Yankees as they came up the hill. Those that survived this would be met by infantry fire at short range. A rout was hoped for and if it came about, Steele was to lead his troop at a charge to finish the job and make victory complete. In the event that the engagement did not go the way of Pegram's planning, the cavalrymen could act as back-up to infantry.

Military matters dealt with, the Colonel had an orderly pour each of his officers a stiff bourbon. Which was used to toast victory. At Rich Mountain and for the South as a whole.

The Ohio and Indiana Yankees hit them the next day – July 11.

From their position at the rear of the defences, Steele and his troopers were unable to see the start of the Union advance. Could only wait and sweat beside their saddled horses: listening to tiny sounds which broke the tense silence after pickets had warned McClellan's men were coming.

Then, at a hand signal from the regular army captain who

86

commanded the artillery, the field guns opened up.

Some of the troopers' horses reared and the men cursed as they fought to calm the spooked animals. A fresh-faced trooper of eighteen named Milton clutched at his stomach, but could not prevent the vomit of fear from exploding from his mouth. Corporal Kershaw crossed himself and snarled: 'Give the bastards hell, boys!' All but one man in their smart, new cavalry uniforms showed tension in varying degrees. The exception was Sergeant Jacobs, who grinned as he met and held the suddenly widened eyes of Steele. Then, raising and lowering his voice in the same cadence as the blasting six-pounders, he said:

'Just like that fight back in the Richmond bar, lieutenant. When you knew it was gonna happen, you was near shakin' scared. Once it got started, wasn't no time to think of anythin' except winnin'.'

Jacobs was right and wrong about the barroom brawl. Steele had not been afraid at any time. But certainly he had not been conscious of any thoughts except the need to triumph once the fists and the bottles and the chairs started to be thrown. It was not an appropriate analogy, anyway. Not for Steele, who had a wide experience of trouble in barrooms. But he allowed that the sergeant, a hard-bitten veteran of fist fights and shooting battles, viewed them both in the same light. A bloodied nose or a bullet in the belly – if the stakes were different, the rewards and penalties should also be diverse.

Steele formed his own mouthline into a smile as he replied: 'We all have to learn, feller. More than can be taught in training camps and at lectures.'

'Right, sir!' the non-com agreed, having to yell now as the gunners found their rhythm and the battery kept up a constant barrage of shellfire which resounded among the ridges like a continuous roll of thunder. He waved his hand towards the source of the deafening din, shrouded in drifting smoke. 'But you don't get a black mark for making a mistake in this! You get dead! Or wounded, which is sometimes worse!'

Steele frowned as the sergeant's expression abruptly matched his talk of death. But then Jacobs was grinning again, his teeth and the whites of his eyes contrasting starkly with his darkened, weathered skin.

'Way I see it, sir, if a man knows there's a good chance he's gonna cash in, he oughta spend the only time that may be left to him enjoyin' himself.'

He drew his Navy Colt, half cocked it, spun the cylinder and slid the revolver back in the holster.

'Fire! Fire at will!'

Steele, Jacobs and the rest of the troop all directed their stares towards the neck of the pass as the artillery barrage was abruptly curtailed and the shrill order was given to the entrenched infantrymen. For long moments, little could be seen clearly through the rolling clouds of evil-smelling black powder smoke. But the crackle of rifle, carbine and musket fire – sounding insignificant after the crashing of the six-pounders – reached the ears of the troopers.

'Mount them, sergeant!' Steele snapped, and swung into his own saddle as rock chips splintered from nearby boulders and twigs snapped among overhead foliage: to reveal that survivors of the artillery fire had raced to within small arms range of the Confederates positions.

'Mount up!' Jacobs yelled and as the order was followed, other sounds reached out from the centre of the battle.

Human voices. Curses of anger and fear. Yells of hysterical glee. Screams of agony. At least a half-dozen bugles sounding the advance.

The smoke from the field-gun barrage was caught and scattered into infinity by a warm breeze that sprang out of the west. And there were gasps, moans and expressions of tacit shock from the mounted men as they received their first clear view of the scene ahead of them.

The living, the dying and the dead. Men running back from the most forward positions, shoulders hunched and heads down. Some dashing straight ahead and others zigzagging. Fleeing from Yankee bullets and in danger of being cut down by the covering fire of their fellow Rebels. Behind them men were sprawled across the heaps of earth displaced by the trench digging: some utterly still and others thrashing about in pain and fear. Men on the run stumbled and fell: stayed down, crawled forward or picked themselves up and continued the panicked flight. There was blood on flesh, uniforms, the earth and the turf.

The men who reached the second line of trenches did not pause, but leapt across them. Yelling words which caused many of the men below them to rise and join the flight.

Not every man who streamed back into the pass clutched a weapon.

Blue-clad figures came into the view of the cavalrymen and when he recalled, later, his first sight of the enemy, Adam Steele admitted to himself that he felt a stab of fear. Perhaps approaching the level of panic which showed in many faces of the retreating front-line defenders. But the terror lasted for no more than a second. Was superseded by an intense anger: directed as much at what he considered the fleeing cowards as towards the triumphantly shrieking attackers.

Some of the Yankees were cut down by the hail of gunfire blasted at them – arms thrown wide, rifles and carbines hurled away as they pitched forward or were bowled over backwards. But each frontrunner who fell was replaced – seemingly by at least three more soldiers.

The shouted orders of Confederate officers could not penetrate the body of sound comprised of gunfire and human voices.

But a bugle blast reached every ear and had the effect of transforming the disorganised rout into an almost orderly regrouping.

Blue- and grey-clad figures continued to exchange gunfire, but with less intensity: each side providing cover for itself while it achieved its next objective. The southerners massing in the area of the timber-log cabin while the northerners consolidated their hard-won ground at the top of the slope.

Orders were given and as a runner with sweat and tears coursing his cheeks raced towards the group of cavalrymen, polished steel flashed in the strong sunlight. Confederate and Union soldiers alike were fixing bayonets.

'Colonel's compliments, sir!' the very young and almost fainting with fear runner shouted. 'Bring your men into the attack at the commencement of close engagement!'

Steele's anger expanded as his estimation of Pegram sank to nothing 'We should hit them first!' he rasped.

Jacobs licked his lips and made to spit, but held the saliva in his mouth as the black eyes of the young lieutenant swung towards him. 'Reckon the colonel's better informed than us, sir,' he said grimly. 'Like about knowin' just how many Yankees are comin' up the hill and in how many directions.'

'But – ' Steele started.

'Beg pardon, sir,' the non-com cut in. 'Easier to turn around and get out if you're standin' still than if you're runnin' into a trap that can close around you.'

The logic of what Sergeant Jacobs had said penetrated into

the younger man's mind despite the rage and frustration which threatened to blind him to reason.

Then bugle calls split the air again, sounding the charge. And blue-uniformed figures swarmed as if composed of a single body into the pass. Infantry and cavalry. From out of the trenches and appearing at the crest of the slope. Yelling, screaming and firing. The muzzle smoke from their guns rising around them and jerking this way and that to the flapping of regimental pennants and the stars and stripes.

'Come on!' Steele bellowed, his unorthodox choice of words for the order coming as the Confederate flag was raised at the centre of the mass of defenders.

Jacobs conveyed the lieutenant's command to the troops with a hand signal and the thud of hoofbeats against springy turf was added to the sounds of the battle.

Because he had heeled his mount into a gallop as he issued the order, Steele was several feet ahead of Jacobs and the other troopers as they closed with the mass of writhing, screaming, cursing foot soldiers. No longer in two separate groups – grey and blue uniforms mixed now as revolvers blasted, bayonets thrust, rifles swung and fists flew.

Steele snatched his carbine from the boot and triggered its single shot. Across the heads of the struggling combatants on the ground. Felt a sense of stupid waste as he saw his bullet spurt blood from the head of a Union cavalryman's horse. The animal skidded to a halt and crumpled to the turf. The rider leapt clear, drawing his sabre and lunging into the throng of hand-to-hand fighters.

The Union man who had been riding immediately behind this one threw his hands to his face, but not before blood could be seen spraying from a hole in his forehead.

'Take that, you sonofabitch!' Jacobs shrieked as the dead Yankee tumbled from his saddle.

Both men slowed their wide-eyed horses, booting their carbines and drawing revolvers. And then Steele felt a release of anger as he made his first kill of a fellow human being – blasting two .36 calibre bullets into the back of a Yankee poised to thrust a bayonet into the belly of a spread-eagled Rebel soldier. In the next instant experienced the depth of fear as death brushed him by – recognising that the whoosh of air across his cheek could only have been caused by a bullet. Glanced over his shoulder as a man screamed, and felt acid bile rise into his

90

throat when he saw blood gushing from the right eye of one of his troopers. Next came shame as, eyes fixed on the scene, he could not even recall the dead man's name as the body tipped from the saddle, the left boot failed to clear the stirrup and the corpse was dragged off by the terrified horse.

Rage again. As he saw in a fleeting glimpse that three more of his men had been hit and unseated from their mounts. Then reined his own horse to a rearing halt and emptied his Colt at the Union cavalry troop. He saw just two hits – one bullet tearing into a shoulder and the other into a chest. Maybe there were more, but he was too intent upon finding a new target after the last to take careful account.

Sergeant Jacobs had already expended his revolver and was heeling his reluctant horse into the struggling foot soldiers – sabre drawn.

There was room in the turmoil of Steele's mind for him to experience resentment bordering on hatred for the way in which his second-in-command had led this new phase of the assault.

But at once the elation of striking at the enemy from close quarters displaced all other emotions within Steele. As he urged his mount in the wake of the veteran sergeant. Cleaved open the skull of a Yankee corporal fumbling to reload his revolver. Then almost severed at the wrists both hands of a private who whirled from killing a Confederate artillery lieutenant with a rifle shot and tried to bayonet the hindquarter of Steele's horse.

The din of battle was like nothing Adam Steele had ever heard before and the crackle of gunfire seemed to be the least of it. Until this moment he would never have believed the human voice-box capable of delivering such a vastly wide range of sound. Expressing agony, rage, terror, delight and perhaps even madness. In every degree.

And he was also aware of the stench of battle. The acrid gunsmoke. The rank smell of animal and human sweat. The sickening rancidity of human waste from dead men and men whose fear caused them to lose control of their bodily functions.

Death and pain were visible on every side. Uniformed figures lay on their backs and on their bellies, curled up into balls or twisted like corkscrews. Some inert and silent, others moving and dumbstruck and more crying for help as they sought positions to ease their agonies. Blood-stained faces, chests, arms, bellies, legs and feet. Flowing still or staunched and already changing from crimson towards black. Here and there some vital organ could be seen between the gory lips of massive wounds. More often, the stark whiteness of bone showed through blood.

Steele slashed with his sabre to the right, then·raised the crimson-dripping blade up and over his horse's neck to attack a blue-clad figure on the left. The big hunter bucked beneath him, spooked by the contact of his hooves with the yielding flesh of the fallen.

During one such switch he saw Sergeant Jacobs open a great wound in the side of a man's neck. Yelled:

'Jacobs!'

But the warning shout was probably not heard. Certainly there was never time for it to be heeded. For a sweating, fat-faced Union infantryman had already released his bayoneted rifle. Aiming it like a lance. With sufficient power for the shining metal to penetrate Jacobs' body from back to front: the red-sheened point emerging at the chest, left of centre.

Steele jerked his horse around and thudded in his heels: his entire being engulfed by a furious temper to a degree which he had never experienced before. The sights and sounds and smells of the Rich Mountain battleground receded into nothing inside his private world: where vengeance was all that mattered. He heard his own breathing and heartbeat and the thud of his mount's hooves. Saw terror grip the fat face of the man he had to kill. Imagined he smelled the sweat oozing from the broad back as the Yankee whirled and lunged into a staggering run.

Bugle calls were sounding again. And men were on the move – the blue and grey uniforms withdrawing from each other and falling back. Shrill-voiced orders were discernible above the lessening noise of a lull in the battle.

Lieutenant Adam Steele saw and heard nothing of this. As, face beaded with sweat and formed into a staring grimace of hatred and rage, he bore down on the fleeing fat man, drew level with him, swung the sabre and leaned to the side.

Like a scythe taking the flower off a stalk, the blade decapi-tated the Yankee. And the severed head bounced on the turf and rolled twenty feet before it came to rest at the base of a tree. By which time the torrent of blood from the neck of the corpse had slowed to an ooze.

Steele reined his mount to a skidding halt that almost un-seated him. And discovered his all-consuming rage suddenly displaced by a bolt of tremendous elation. Which in turn was superseded by an almost uncontrollable need to be sick as he looked down at the mask of terror which was the face of the severed head lying no more than six feet from him.

'Beg pardon, sir!' a man shouted and when Steele looked away from the ghastly object at the foot of the tree, he saw that the runner on the other side of his horse had obviously tried to get his attention before. It was the same youthful soldier who had delivered the message at the opening of the battle. But now he looked many years older. 'Colonel's compliments, sir. We are about to withdraw. Colonel requests you provide covering fire, sir.'

Steele shifted his gaze to the centre of the battlefield and saw that he had pursued Jacobs' killer more than three hundred yards away from the area where the main carnage had been wrought. Now there was an interlude in the slaughter, as the survivors and walking wounded on both sides attended to those unable to help themselves.

By common consent of Yankees and Rebels, the centre of the battleground had become neutral territory, where each side allowed the other to move freely and unhindered on missions of mercy. While, to the left and right of where Steele acknowledged the runner with a salute, a more superior force of Union soldiers prepared for a second assault against the demoralised Confederates who were fixing to withdraw.

As he urged his mount forward, he made a rough estimate of the number of his troopers who had clustered into a group, their expressions as dejected as any. Thirty at least. But no more than thirty five.

He pushed his blood-run sabre into the scabbard and reloaded his carbine, hands shaking. Fifteen to twenty men lost. Including his guide and mentor, Sergeant Dwight Jacobs. Maybe not all of them dead, but those that were being loaded into supply wagons converted to hospital ambulances were out of the fight.

'What a friggin' awful mess, sir,' a trooper named Nash muttered.

'We lost Sergeant Jacobs,' Trooper Rodell added dully.

'The lieutenant knows that!' Corporal Kershaw snarled.

'Harry Milton as well,' Rodell went on in a choked-up voice. 'Belly ripped open by a bayonet. I could see like all worms crawlin' inside of him.'

Steele recalled that Milton was the boy who was sick when the artillery pieces started to fire.

'Sir?' Kershaw posed, anxiety in his voice and face as he saw the absent expression on the lieutenant's face.

'Right, corporal!' Steele replied sharply and raked his suddenly hard eyes over the faces of all his men. 'You take over the sergeant's duties. You men, count your blessings, not the dead. But this thing isn't ended yet.'

But the struggle for Rich Mountain was, in the sense of a pitched battle. For the main body of Confederate soldiers were able to pull out with their dead and wounded before the Union men were ready to mount a follow-up attack. And Steele was able to move his troopers in their wake with just a desultory exchange of fire.

'If this is war, lieutenant,' Trooper Nash growled as sounds of pursuit faded and Steele signalled a halt and dismount, 'you can friggin' keep it.'

The junior officer climbed wearily to the ground in the wooded glade and looked around at his men. Just as he had noticed that the runner had seemed to age during the battle, so now the younger members of his troop looked a lot older than he remembered them. Thinner, too. With hollow eyes and sunken cheeks. Even smaller as they hunched their shoulders, some of them clutching their hands together as if they were cold. Here and there a man shook. It was impossible to visualise them as the same troop which had ridden so proudly out from Richmond a few days ago.

'I don't want it, trooper,' Steele rasped through pursed lips. 'And we're not alone in that. But I reckon all of us are stuck with it.'

CHAPTER SIX

PRIVATE Elliot Cox from South Bend, Indiana was through with war. A lanky, good-looking eighteen-year-old with dark eyes and a mop of curly black hair he had never wanted any part of it. But his father and his elder brother had branded him a coward for failing to volunteer at the earliest opportunity. And after George Cox and most of the other men of military service age had left South Bend to answer the call to arms, even his girl had turned against him.

So he went to the enlistment centre and he joined, hopeful that his experience as a sales clerk in his family's clothing store would ensure him a safe job in administration or supply. But the Union army already had more clerks than it needed and thus it was that Elliot Cox found himself running up to the Rich Mountain pass clutching a Springfield musket and mouthing a prayer. He never fired the gun before he lost it and his prayer was answered.

He thought for a moment that he was about to die, when he tripped over the outstretched leg of a fallen comrade and pitched to the ground, crashing his forehead against a rock hidden in long grass. The pain was like nothing he had ever experienced, but it lasted for only a moment before he plunged into unconsciousness.

His head still hurt, as he wandered aimlessly through the Alleghany Mountains and sometimes he touched the centre of the pain – felt the crusted blood of the wound. But he could live with the pain now that he had escaped from the battleground and was free of the war.

Not of its memories. They would take time to fade. It had only been part of a day and a single night since he regained consciousness, threw up at the scene before his newly opened eyes, and crawled away from its horrors.

'Hold it, Yankee!'

Elliot Cox was brought to such an abrupt halt by the snarled command that his upper body still had momentum and he almost toppled to the ground. Swaying, he snapped his head to right and left and even glanced over his shoulder: unable to decide from which direction the voice had spoken.

Then twigs snapped and foliage rustled. And two grey-uniformed figures moved out of a clump of brush six feet in front of him.

'I ain't – ' he started to say.

'Shut up!' the Rebel to the left growled.

'Hands in the air, kid. Way up.'

The one on the right was a thirty-year-old corporal with ears that stuck out and suspicious-green eyes. The trooper looked almost as afraid as Cox as his dark eyes moved constantly in their sockets: peering to left and right at the surrounding trees as if he expected a whole army of Union soldiers to appear while the non-com advanced on the prisoner. Both men held levelled carbines.

'You on your own?' the trooper, who was in his early twenties, asked.

'Easy, Nash,' Corporal Kershaw growled, having seen the fear erupt in the young trooper when they first heard sound of the lone man approaching through the timber. Hearing the quaver in his voice as he spoke now. 'Only company he's got is us. Go bring the lieutenant back here.'

'You sure I should leave and – '

'Friggin' civilians!' Kershaw rasped and raised his voice to snarl: 'Do as you're damn well told, trooper!'

Nash nodded, spun around and made haste to comply with the order.

'That's what I am, sir,' the Yankee private blurted. 'A civilian. It was my folks and my girl made me – '

'But you been in the army long enough to know you don't call a corporal sir!' Kershaw cut in as he halted with the muzzle of the Sharps less than twelve inches away from the rapidly rising and falling chest of Cox. 'Unbutton your holster and ease out the revolver, kid.'

'Yes, sir. I mean corporal.'

Kershaw noticed for the first time that the youngster wore

gloves. Black buckskin, of the type that many officers affected. Still shiny with newness. The left gloved hand reached around to unfasten the holster flap while the right one came up to take hold of the Colt butt.

'I ain't army anymore, corporal. I deserted. After the fightin' back there.' He raised his left hand, thumb extended, to point over his shoulder. 'I didn't do no shootin' at your people. I tripped and fell. Over somebody's leg. Got knocked out. When I come to, I saw that leg wasn't fixed to somebody anymore. Must've been blown off by a shell. Saw another guy with a hole right through his chest. Big enough to put two fists through . . .'

Jack Kershaw had been in the army since he was eighteen but had never seen active service until Rich Mountain. For he was always assigned to posts on the eastern seaboard, mostly engaged on clerical duties. He was an orderly at the West Point Military Academy when the siege of Sumter made war inevitable. And because he was a native of South Carolina, he had sided with the Confederacy.

As he listened to the Yankee with crusted blood on his brow catalogue the horrors of mutilation he had witnessed in the aftermath of the Union's opening assault on the Rich Mountain pass, memories of similar sights – seen at first hand – crowded into Kershaw's mind. And for the stretched second it took him to snap: 'Deserters should be shot!' he screwed his eyes tight shut.

The act of closing his eyes served to draw a veil over the recollections of bleeding and broken bodies. But the process took too long. And the threat implicit in the words he spoke was ill-conceived.

Elliot Cox was on the point of releasing the big .45 Army Colt. Feeling better by the moment. Fear gone and the pain in his head almost completely diminished. As he reflected that capture by the Rebels was the perfect solution to the trap he walked into when he escaped from the battlefield horrors. A trap which he had been unaware of until now: previously had experienced only euphoria at being free. But he could never have been free. He could not have gone home or back to the army. And wherever else he went he would have been in constant danger of capture and disgrace. Or worse.

But capture of this kind – by the enemy – was his way out. For there was no dishonour in being a prisoner of war. Especially a wounded prisoner of war. And no matter how bad the conditions in Confederate prisons, they would be far away from the fighting and killing.

Then the man had said *deserters should be shot.* A man who was a soldier. Aiming a carbine at him. And Elliot Cox came down from the highest peak of joy to the depths of depression. Tightened his grip on the Colt butt, tilted up the barrel, cocked the hammer and squeezed the trigger.

'No!' he screamed. And the shrill cry put to panicked flight a flock of birds from the tops of the surrounding trees.

This as Corporal Jack Kershaw died on his feet with a .45 calibre bullet in his heart: the carbine slipping from his spasming hands as his legs went limp and he crumpled to the grass.

Cox said, 'No,' again, the word little more than an escape of breath from between his trembling lips. His whole body trembled while he witnessed the dying of the man. And the bright crimson stain that blossomed on the grey uniform tunic of Kershaw triggered fresh memories of the horrific scenes which had caused him to come to this place.

He whirled and ran. Unaware that the Colt had dropped from his shaking fingers. His mind still filled with images of shattered human flesh and crawling rivulets of blood. He could even hear the sounds of battle. So clearly defined they seemed to be crashing and reverberating in the here and now.

'He killed him! The Yankee bastard killed him!'

The sounds which Elliot Cox heard were not created inside his head. For Lieutenant Adam Steele and Troopers Nash and Rodell also heard the crash, whistle and detonation of artillery fire as they lunged out of the high brush and skidded to a halt ten feet from where Corporal Jack Kershaw lay crumpled in the total inertia of obvious death. The barrage having opened up no more than two seconds after the revolver shot cracked.

Beyond where the dead man lay, his killer was racing for the cover of trees on the far side of the clearing.

'We'll be dead, too, we don't get the frig outta here!' Rodell yelled.

It was a reasonable, if not copy-book-style estimation of the military situation. For the artillery barrage was coming from the direction in which the lone Yankee soldier was running. Was being laid by a Union battery and aimed at the Confederates who had withdrawn from Rich Mountain. Albeit the gunners were firing blind, arcing their shells across heavily wooded mountain terrain. But some of the shots were smashing down through the trees dangerously close to the clearing.

Although not deaf to the din, Adam Steele was temporarily oblivious to the cause and effect. As he looked from the dead Kershaw to the fleeing man and felt himself suffused by the white heat of uncontrollable temper.

He had lost another trooper. More wastefully than those who had fallen at Rich Mountain. It was Kershaw's own fault he had died. Nash's blurted report of the capture and the fact that the corporal's carbine was still cocked where it lay on the grass was evidence of this. But Steele felt compelled to accept a portion of the blame. He was Kershaw's commanding officer and should have ensured the man – and every man in his troop – knew how to handle such a situation.

He unbuttoned his holster flap as Nash and Rodell hurled themselves to the ground and pressed their hands to their heads.

Kershaw was a career soldier.

Steele drew the Navy Colt.

A whistling sound changed its note to a hiss. Branches snapped. A twelve-pounder shell impacted with the ground and exploded a crater less than forty feet away.

Steele was an officer because of privilege. Just like Cliff Gordon had accused.

He cocked the hammer of the revolver.

'Lieutenant, let's get the hell outta here!'

It was Nash who screamed the demand. Not long ago, the same fresh-faced trooper had said at Rich Mountain: *What a friggin' awful mess.* That was right. About the battle and the urgent, haphazard preparations for the battle.

Adam Steele, rich man's son, given leadership of men like Kershaw and Nash and Rodell and Milton. And Sergeant Dwight Jacobs. Picked out of a bar-room brawl by . . . His anger became redirected at a new target. Major Miles Vernon. A veteran leader who should have been here. Instead was doubtless still back in Richmond. Selecting potential officers with little more thought than it took to stick a pin in a list of names.

He levelled the gun at a visible target. Squeezed the trigger.

Another artillery shell exploded. Less than thirty feet away. To the left instead of the right this time.

Steele was a crackshot with a rifle and an expert with a shotgun. The Navy Colt bucked in his hand. The running man screamed and went down, blood spurting from a wound in the back of his right thigh.

'Let's go, lieutenant!'

It was Rodell this time. Steele ignored the plea and lunged forward. Racing across the clearing as the Yankee struggled to crawl into the trees. He cocked the revolver as he closed with the wounded Elliot Cox who, in the turmoil of his enraged mind, represented every cruel twist of fate which had caused Adam Steele to be here.

The young man from South Bend rolled over on to his back, tears streaming across his cheeks, gloved hands stretching up towards the Confederate cavalry lieutenant who came to a halt beside him.

'He was gonna kill –'

Steele, his face dark with fury and his black eyes glinting as if there were chips of shiny metal in them, curled back his lips and squeezed the trigger of the gun. Cox screamed as the bullet tore into his belly, stretching his body to the limits of the tendons. The gun was cocked again and fired again. This bullet opened a hole in the helpless victim's right cheek and he died. But Steele blasted three more shots at the corpse, to empty the chambers of live shells.

He smelt the pungent taint of burnt powder and licked the sweat of tension off his upper lip. Heard both Nash and Rodell yelling at him. And the crashing of the artillery barrage.

When the handgun clicked empty, he dropped to his knees and began pistol-whipping the unfeeling face of what once had been Elliot Cox. Felt hands gripping and tugging at him.

'He's dead, sir!'

'You can't hurt him no more! We gotta go, lieutenant!'

He wrenched his head around and the fury of his expression seemed to have a palpable driving force which sent the two troopers staggering back from him.

Then the terrible anger was gone and he felt near to exhaustion from the unconscious effort it had taken to sustain it. He shifted his suddenly dull-eyed gaze from the horrified and frightened faces of his own men to the pulpy mess that was all that was left of the Union private's features. Then glimpsed his own hands, which were dripping with the blood which had splashed from the wounds.

'Dear, dear God!' he rasped.

'Please, sir. The Yankees'll be here soon as the guns stop.'

'Sure, trooper,' he told the anxious Nash. 'Get the body of the corporal and return to base.'

As he spoke he struggled to pull the buckskin gloves off the dead hands. Hurriedly donned them himself. Failing to take note of the tag inside the right glove which was stamped with the legend: MADE BY COX AND SONS, SOUTH BEND, INDIANA.

Blood squelched inside them, but he could no longer see the incriminating colour staining his hands. He snatched up the discarded revolver and whirled as he rose from the ground. Nash and Rodell were on the other side of the clearing, struggling to lift the dead weight of Corporal Kershaw.

A shell whistled and hissed. Tree branches snapped. Leaves fell.

'Down!' he yelled, and half turned in the direction from which the sounds came.

And hurled himself to the ground in unison with the two troopers.

The twelve-pounder hit the centre of the clearing and blasted a deep crater: scattered the debris far and wide. Turf and clods of earth from beneath the grass. Steele was pressed to the ground, sideways on to the point of impact some thirty feet to his right.

Blast tugged at him. Soil rained on him. A clod of earth with a pound weight piece of time-smoothed rock smashed down on to the back of his skull.

'The lieutenant's bought it!' Rodell yelled when the sound of the shell's impact was reduced to a ringing in the ears and the final grain of displaced earth had fallen.

Nash took his hands off the top of his head and gazed across the clearing through the drifting smoke at the unmoving Adam Steele. Who, except for his right arm and left foot, was entirely covered with dirt.

'The best way there could be, for us,' he growled as he eased up to his feet. 'Seems like he's dead and buried both.'

CHAPTER SEVEN

LIEUTENANT Adam Steele wondered if Charlie Grady had been among the Union soldiers killed at Rich Mountain. Then considered the possibility that the husband of the Richmond rooming-house keeper might even have been one of the blue-uniformed men he brought down with a gunshot or a blow with the sabre.

He grimaced. It would not have been pleasant knowledge to live with. But he had to think about something in the total darkness – and try as he might, he could not dislodge images of death from his mind. And reflecting on long shots caused him less anguish than recalling what had actually happened: the most insistent of such memories being his brutal, mindless murder of the young Yankee soldier from South Bend, Indiana.

No, not murder! The country was at war with itself and Steele and the kid were on different sides.

'Who is this man Grady, Adam?' a voice asked.

For a seeming eternity, Steele had existed in a black world between waking and sleeping and was never quite sure whether he was dreaming or had control over his thought processes. He knew he recognised the voice but could not put a name to the man who spoke the words. Kershaw? Milton? Jacobs? A kid of not yet twenty who had once said a few words to Steele . . . just before he lost his face?

The face didn't matter. Once he put his mind to discovering the name, the face would match. But he felt too tired to make the effort. The familiar voice had spoken in a dream, waking him, and now he sought to sink into sleep again.

'Adam? Adam, please say something.'

Diana! He recognised the voice of his dark-haired fiancée instantly.

'I think . . . '

Now he had the man. It was his father.

He completed the movement of his head which had signalled to Ben Steele that his son was conscious.

Diana gasped: 'Oh, Adam, my darling.'

'I can't see you,' he told them and to his own ears his voice sounded as weak as he felt.

'What's that, son?'

'He says he can't see us, Mr Steele,' the woman explained. 'We know, Adam. Your head's all bandaged. Including your eyes, my poor darling.'

She began to cry, softly.

'Where . . . ? What . . . ? How long . . . ?'

Steele at first experienced a deep sense of satisfaction at having identified his two visitors. Then, just as fleeting, a surge of love for them and joy that they were nearby. Now there was only a demanding curiosity as he clung to reality – which was almost self-defeating as the effort this required threatened to exhaust him into unconsciousness again. But his father's voice gave him something substantial to which he could fasten his tenuous mental grip.

'Don't you know anything, son?'

'I killed some men . . . lost some.'

Diana sobbed, but quietened when Ben Steele spoke soft, consoling words which his son did not catch. But for a few moments, other sounds penetrated into his dark world. Voices, footfalls, the squeaking of an unoiled wheel. Even birdsong. Then his father said:

'You're in the Chimborazo Hospital at Richmond, my boy. You fought at the battle of Rich Mountain. The Confederates had to withdraw into the Alleghanies and you and your troop were detailed to protect the rear. But you had a foul stroke of luck. A Union shell landed close by and you got a blow to the head. Severe concussion is how the doctors here classify what resulted.'

In some instances, Adam Steele's recollections of the past were clearer in dreams than when he was awake. Now, as his father spoke, he received some memories as fresh as if he had never reviewed them before.

'Two of your men were with you. They fetched help and you were taken forward. But there wasn't the time or facilities for wounded men to be treated. The Union army was too close on

103

the heels of your group. So your commanding officer . . . '

He obviously could not recall the name.

'Colonel Pegram,' his son supplied.

'That's the man,' Ben Steele said, obviously pleased that Adam had contributed a positive response. 'He sent you and those like you back from the lines while he tried to make a stand. And I guess you can consider yourself lucky, my boy. Two days after the wounded were despatched, Pegram was forced to surrender his entire command or risk – '

'How long, Pa?' Adam asked.

'Almost three weeks ago now. You've been here in this bed, unconscious for most of the time, for fifteen days. Reckon the doctors will be real pleased to hear you're coherent at last.'

'We surely are, Adam,' Diana said tearfully, and he felt the weight of her hand on his through the bedcovers.

'Why are my eyes covered?' he asked and felt his stomach churn with a fear greater than that he could remember feeling before the Rich Mountain battle.

'That's nothing to worry about, son,' his father assured, too quickly and obviously deeply concerned. 'A blow to the head like you took can have all kinds of effects. The doctors felt it best your eyes be rested.'

'A chance I've been blinded?'

The fear was weakening him still further. He could feel it in every part of his body and hear it in his whispered words.

'No!' Diana blurted shrilly in a tone that made it clear she was not answering his questions.

'A chance, son,' his father said grimly. 'But equally there's a chance your eyes will be as good as ever. We are praying everything will be all right, Adam. And when that's seen to be so, we want you to have done with this war. There'll be no problem although you'll be fully fit again and suitable for active service. I've spoken to some people. An honourable discharge on grounds of ill-health can be arranged. Diana has told me you proposed to her the day before you left home. I'm delighted by that. And so is Diana's father. We've discussed it. We think you two young people should be married as soon as possible. Then go out West. California or Oregon, maybe. It could happen you'll put down roots out there. If not, you can come back east as soon as this trouble is over.'

Despite being close to total exhaustion, Adam Steele felt the heat of anger spread from the pit of his stomach. And realised that it showed on the lower half of his face below the bandages when he heard Diana caution:

'Please, Mr Steele. Not now.'

'Listen, son,' his father insisted, his tone revealing his deep concern. 'The situation is becoming very serious. McClellan routed your people around Beverly and the Union have a firm hold on western Virginia now. The Union had a major set back up near Manassas Junction in a fight they're calling the Battle of Bull Run. By God, boy, those engagements were picnics compared with what's going to happen in the future.' His voice was rising now and as his anger expanded, so that of his son's lost its edge. 'And picnic is the right word for Bull Run! The Washington smart set actually rode out in buggies and carriages with food hampers to watch the damn fighting!'

'I'll have to ask you to keep your voice down, sir,' a stranger to Adam Steele said sternly. 'This is a hospital ward. Time anyway, for you to leave your son to his rest.'

'I'm sorry,' Ben Steele croaked. 'A minute or so longer, please?'

'Very well. Then you really must go. And the lady, too.'

Adam sensed his father leaning closer to him, then felt his breath on his cheek. 'Are you still listening, son?'

'Yes, Pa. But I don't think – '

'Please hear me out?' Only on the night he rushed from the big house to follow the Keysville men to Richmond had Adam Steele heard such a tone of urgent pleading in his father's voice. He did not wait for a response before he continued: 'You saw and did terrible things at Rich Mountain. As did everyone there and at Bull Run. But there's worse – much worse – to come. War is a trade for experienced men. And there just aren't enough of them around. It's stupid that you, a green lieutenant, should have been given command of fifty equally raw men. But you're not unique. Among your people and on the Union side, the only opportunity there's going to be to train such men is to throw them into battle. And those battles are going to become harder, more brutal and vastly more costly in terms of human life. Get out, son. Take Diana and move far away from the slaughter.'

'Pa, I – '

'One final point, son,' Ben Steele cut in and, for the first time as his father laid a hand on his shoulder, the younger man realised the elder was on the other side of the bed from Diana.

'The South will lose. A battle here and there may go their way, but that will only serve to prolong the tragedy of this criminal war. In time, the might of the Union will surely crush the South.'

'You through, Pa?' Adam Steele croaked.

He heard his father swallow hard, then sigh. The shuffle of his boot soles as he straightened up beside the bed. 'Yes, son. Words are all I have in this situation and I reckon I've used all I have.'

'Grateful to you.' He moved his head on the pillow. 'And to you, Diana. For coming here to see me. And for your concern.'

'Oh, darling, please – '

'Allow him his say, child,' Ben Steele urged.

'I've said my thanks. Like to say, too, that I respect your opinion. And your loyalty to your chosen side. But I'm committed to oppose you.' Diana began to cry again, but Adam Steele continued, only pausing to suck breath into his weary body. 'Just need to give you a warning, Pa. That if you ever come to see me again – here or anywhere else I happen to be – and try to subvert *my* loyalties from the Confederate cause, I'll see you are arrested as – '

Diana Summers' sobs became an elongated wail.

'Sir, madam!' the man who had chided the visitors earlier snapped.

'Yes, we're leaving,' Ben Steele answered in a resigned tone. Then: 'Come my dear.' He applied a light pressure to his son's shoulder and whispered. 'Jim Bishop and Elroy send their best. Good luck to you, Adam.'

Their footfalls sounded and receded. The man they left lying immobile under the white covers of the bed in the large, bright and airy hospital ward felt the salt dampness of tears soak into the soft dressing which masked his eyes. Then he sank into a dreamless sleep.

For a further three weeks he remained where he was, experiencing a gradual improvement in his condition. He slept now, rather than slipping into periods of unconsciousness. And there were clear dividing lines between sleeping and waking. He was able to sit up and be fed with solids instead of drawing nourishment from liquids poured into him through a tube inserted down his throat. He could think lucidly most of the time and join in conversations with other wounded soldiers who shared the ward. Three weeks after the harrowing visit from his father and Diana, there was the traumatic experience of

106

having the bandages removed from his head. And for a few short seconds the world was a joyful place when he realised he could see – as clearly as before, after the short period of adjustment from pitch darkness to August sunlight was over.

But then into his range of vision came sights of the other men in the Chimborazo Hospital ward. Men without arms or legs. Men with terrible disfigurements. Men who were whole in body but who stared directly ahead and said nothing, obviously as unthinking as vegetables. Most of them of an age with Steele or younger. And as he found the strength to walk and strolled the hospital corridors and grounds to build his strength still further, he saw other wards lined with beds in which similarly broken young men lay.

What talk there was among the patients in the Chimborazo war wards was mostly of a personal nature: the men concerned only with reliving their own experiences and uninterested in discussing the ever-changing military and political situation which had ensued after they were wounded.

But regular copies of the *Richmond Examiner* delivered to the hospital kept the eager-for-knowledge Steele abreast of what was happening. While from old copies he learned the details of how the Union had secured the western section of the state and of the incredible series of blunders by both sides which had ended with General Joe Johnston and his armies of the Shenandoah and Potomac routing McDowell's Union army at Bull Run.

Since that debacle which many Southern sympathisers had mistakenly assumed won them total victory of the war, both the Union and Confederacy appeared to be licking their wounds – making plans to avoid such costly mistakes in the future. Never again, the reading public was informed, would untrained troops be thrown into a battle in a manner which led to almost five thousand of them being killed.

Sporadic fighting continued. On August 10, the Union army was defeated at Wilson's Creek in the state of Missouri. And ten days later the Union garrison at Lexington in the same state fell to the Confederates. But these two victories did not win the state as a whole for the south.

Along the coastline, the blockade of Confederate seaports ordered by Abraham Lincoln was mostly ineffective because there were too many harbours and not enough ships to guard them. So vital imports from France and Great Britain were continuing to reach the supply-hungry south.

Apart from dizzy spells which were likely to attack him unexpectedly, Lieutenant Adam Steele went from strength to strength. And when he was discharged from hospital at the end of August and ordered to report to command headquarters in the city, he looked forward eagerly to taking an active part in the army's efforts to prepare for the long, hard struggle that surely lay ahead.

But found himself assigned to light duties in the administration of supplies. Became a clerk in uniform working at a desk. And soon came to detest his senior officers and the non-coms and enlisted men who without exception made it known that he should share their feelings of relief at such an easy – and safe – tour of duty.

During the remainder of the year and into early 1862, as the dizzy spells became less frequent and then stopped altogether, he signed forms and shuffled papers. While other men received thorough training in warfare and many continued to experience the real thing.

The Union was defeated at Ball's Buff, Virginia and a Yankee Brigadier General with the imposing name of Ulysses S. Grant lost Belmont Missouri to the Rebels. Then came the first of a series of set-backs for the South when the Union captured Port Royal in South Carolina.

From January 19 in the New Year until March 14 reports from the various fronts seemed constantly bad for the South. Especially along the three-hundred-mile-long defensive line stretching from the Mississippi River in the west to Cumberland Gap on the Virginia border. Mill Springs, Kentucky was lost. Fort Henry on the Tennessee River. And Ulysses S. Grant gained promotion to major-general when he captured Fort Donalson, Tennessee along with fifteen thousand prisoners. Nashville was abandoned by the Rebels. Meanwhile, west and north of the main offensive, the Union won the battle of Pea Ridge, Arkansas and New Madrid, Missouri was left for the Yankees to take without resistance. And thus did the maverick state of Missouri come within the fold of the Union.

Virtually the only cheering news for the South was the fact that the Confederate ironclad *Merrimack* had beaten off an attack by the Union ship *Monitor* in Hampton Roads north of Norfolk Virginia and was in command of the mouth of the James River.

Steele read avidly those official army reports that came his way and continued to scour the *Richmond Examiner* and any other newspaper he was able to lay hands on. Itching to escape the confinement of office walls and make restitution, by positive action, for the errors he considered he had made at Rich Mountain.

But he had quickly stopped making his disenchantment with his duty known among his fellow pen-pushers and paper-shufflers at headquarters. Learning that a mere lieutenant was in the same situation as the lowliest private as regards a duty he found disagreeable – complaining earned him nothing except unpopularity among those around him. And, more importantly, those above him.

So he gritted his teeth and stuck it out. And had his patience rewarded on the morning of March 24, the day after Stonewall Jackson lost the first battle for the Shenandoah Valley at Kernstown, when he was ordered to report to Captain Joel Hood at the Richmond railroad depot – with his horse and equipment.

He was given three hours to meet the order and was at the station in less than half that time. Three trains, with lines of both passenger and enclosed freight cars behind the locomotives, were waiting at the station. Steele was the only army man in the small depot café where he drank coffee and listened to the talk among brakemen while the engine crews built up steam on their footplates.

'We sure are takin' one hell of a damn hidin' out in Tennessee,' an elderly railroadman growled, his accent revealing that he was talking about his home state.

'You from there, Joe?' a much younger brakeman asked.

'Sure enough am, son. Hopeful there'll be time after we delivered the fightin' men where they're goin' for me to visit the old place where I was born and growed up.'

'Where is the end of the line this trip?' the younger man asked.

'Things like that are secret, son,' the old-timer replied, with a glance towards where Steele sat.

The young lieutenant showed a familiar grin. No longer foolish, for just as he had noticed in others, the violent and bloody action at Rich Mountain had aged his features. And now the grin acted to negate this effect and made him look his true age. 'Won't be seeing Lincoln for awhile. So there's no chance of me letting anything slip while he and I take tea, feller.'

The old-timer slapped a thigh and laughed. 'Reckon not, lieutenant.' He turned back to the young brakeman. 'Well, son, if what I heard is true, we're gonna turn around and come back from a place in Mississippi called Corinth. Where our passengers go after that, I ain't got no idea. Just hope, like I say, I get the chance to go north a few miles. Over the state line and see my old home.'

'Where's that?' The young brakeman was losing interest now, peering out of the café's greasy window to where a column of cavalrymen were entering the depot.

'Little dot on the map called Shiloh, son.'

'Never heard of it, Joe.'

'Few folks have, son. And ain't no reason why they ever should.'

The younger railroadman had risen from his chair and gone to the door, dragging a lame left leg to show why he was not in military uniform. While the elder one sighed, lit a pipe into which he had been tamping tobacco, and gazed eagerly at Adam Steele.

'You chase them Yankees outta Tennessee, lieutenant. Kentucky and all points north, too. I'm sure you will.'

'God willing,' Steele told him.

The old man shook his head. 'No, son. God has nothing to do with it. War is the Devil's province.'

Steele stood up and glanced out of the window to where the cavalrymen had halted and were dismounting, their uniforms freshly pressed and their buttons and weapons gleaming. And saw, superimposed on this present scene, a vivid image of the blood and the gore and the broken bodies in the pass at Rich Mountain.

'It sure is hell,' he allowed.

CHAPTER EIGHT

'RIGHT, lieutenant,' Captain Joel Hood rasped through teeth clenched and bared in a grin. 'Get the men mounted and ready to go kill our share of bluebellies.'

'Mount up!' Steele shouted, his voice ringing out clearly against the distant crackle of gunfire. And displayed a grin of his own when the sixty-five troopers and non-coms cheered as they complied with the order.

It was a little after nine on the morning of Sunday, April 6 and the battle that was destined to go down in history as 'Bloody Shiloh' had been raging since dawn: when the first wave of Confederates had launched themselves towards the Union encampment in the vicinity of Shiloh Church.

All night the troopers had been camped in a stand of timber on a dirt trail called Hamburg River Road which ran parallel at this point with a trickling Tennessee River tributary known as Lick Creek. And throughout the mostly sleepless night, while Hood was in conference at Major-General Braxton Bragg's headquarters and Steele was in command of the men, he sensed the tension mounting. And endured a high degree of it himself: readily admitting that this was caused by his dislike of the onus of responsibility – as, from far off, the night was disturbed at intervals by exchanges of gunfire between Union pickets and Rebel skirmishers.

On the train from Richmond to the Army of Mississippi supply point at Corinth he had gotten to know a little and respect a lot the forty-year-old regular army officer to whom he had been assigned. For Hood was a tall, gaunt-faced, balding man of the kind who inspired confidence in his men. An officer, Boston born, who had been on the staff of Robert E. Lee and had thrown in his lot with the Confederacy simply because of his admiration for the famous general. And having made the choice pledged unwavering loyalty to the cause and had faith without vanity in his ability to do what was asked of him.

On the train ride, too, and during the pause at Corinth followed by the advance north from Mississippi into Tennessee, Steele had been made aware that the entire troop felt the same as he about Captain Hood. But had little respect for their lieutenant: this view shared by both the regular army troopers and the volunteers who were as new to military service as Steele was.

But Hood ran a tight troop and no man in it dared to show open disdain for the young junior officer. But it was undoubtedly present and although it remained surreptitious, and was never more apparent than during the pre-dawn and early morning daylight hours of that Sunday while command of the troop was delegated to Steele.

Perhaps, he was to reflect later, because he allowed his anxiety to show – his concern triggered by the fact that, since his assignment to Hood he had become comfortably used to have a superior officer close at hand. Just as, back on the Steele Plantation, his decision making had been tempered by the nearby influence of his father.

But such academic self-examination had no place in his mind as dawn broke on that April Sunday in 1862 and he heard the sounds of gunfire swell from the sparodic crackle of scattered skirmishes to the cacophony of full-scale battle.

He wanted to fight. God how he wanted to attack the enemy who had killed Kershaw and Milton and Jacobs and who had maimed or driven out of their minds the men he saw in Chimborazo Hospital. For all those days, weeks and months he had been forced to kick his heels in the Richmond office of supply he had craved for this day to arrive. But he wanted no part of decision making: listened to the sounds of guns blasting and men shouting and silently prayed for Hood to return to the Hamburg River Road. Because Hood had the experience and the rank: and it was his responsibility to make the decisions and give the orders which would undoubtedly lead to at least some of the troops being killed or as badly wounded as the men in the hospital at Richmond.

And Joel Hood had returned, his appearance flooding Steele with relief. Which gave way to an almost euphoric eagerness to enter the battle as he sat his horse alongside the captain, while

Sergeant James Perry yelled at the troopers to form into double rank facing the officers.

The morning was overcast and the light was dull beneath the overhanging foliage of the tall oak trees. But uniform buttons and oiled firearms, polished harness brass and hat badges had a smart sheen against grey fabric and the curried coats of the mounts.

The cheering was over now and the men were attentive – this attitude in combination with their smartness seen by Steele as a fine example of what could be achieved by an officer able to impose discipline on enlisted men without attracting resentment.

Hood nodded his approval of what he saw and continued to rake his dark eyes back and forth over the twin rows of faces as he said: 'We have them on the run, men. And if things keep going the way they are, we'll have the beating of them by nightfall. But there's a bunch of obstinate bluebellies further along this road who are holding up the advance. We've been given the job of aiding the men who are right now trying to shift the Yankees. So let's go get them, uh!'

There was another cheer, which lost impetus and came to an end as the order to turn and move forward was passed from Hood through Steele to Perry who roared it at the men. And then there was just the clop of hooves and the creak of harness as the column of troopers rode out of the timber and swung north along the Hamburg River Road, leaving Lick Creek at their backs.

'Glad to see me, weren't you, lieutenant?' Hood asked as he and Steele rode side by side at the head of the double line of men.

'Sir?'

'No need to be ashamed of it. I'm damn glad Anderson has told me what to do. Just like he's happy to have Bragg further up the chain of command and Bragg can blame General Johnston if things go wrong. Who knows, maybe Johnston figures that all he's doing is what Jefferson Davis wants.'

'Sir, I – ' Steele began, discomfited by the ease and accuracy with which Hood had judged his secret fears. And, as became clear when the captain interrupted him, his hopes as well.

'I asked to have you assigned to me after talking with Major Miles Vernon, lieutenant. And some other people who were at Rich Mountain. Knew I could be sentencing you to death or putting you in line to lose an arm or a leg maybe. But you volunteered, didn't you?'

Steele had recovered from the surprise – used the action of pulling on Elliot Cox's gloves to avoid looking at Hood. 'Yes, sir,' he acknowledged.

'But it wouldn't have mattered if you were a conscript, lieutenant. The war's here to be fought and we have to fight it. Army men like me and civilians in uniform like yourself. Lot of us have already been killed and many more will die before it's over. The ones with the best chance of surviving are those that don't get involved – if you get my drift, Lieutenant?'

'I think so, sir.'

'Involved with their men and with their feelings – towards their men and about themselves. So just follow orders, Mr Steele. And if it falls to you to originate orders, do the best you can under the prevailing conditions – with your only consideration the advancement of the cause for which you are fighting.'

'Grateful to you, Captain.'

A nod. 'I understand you used to engage in field sports, lieutenant. May help you to think of war in that context. With the enemy your quarry and the men under you as the hounds. The best damn pack in the county, so deserving of good treatment and respect.'

'It's a thought, sir.'

'Used well, a highly trained pack of hounds can achieve fine kills. But it has to be directed. Unselfishly.'

He looked hard into Steele's profile and the power of his gaze forced the younger man to look at him.

'Sir?'

Hood was grimly serious. 'While you are under my command, lieutenant, you will not go tearing off hell for leather in pursuit of personal vengeance.'

Steele swallowed hard, wondering which incident the cavalry captain had heard about. Hood supplied the answer.

'At Rich Mountain you abandoned your position as leader of a troop to pursue and behead an enemy soldier who killed one of your men. If I witness you do anything of that nature, I will either shoot you down or ensure that you face court martial for dereliction of duty under fire. One man is of no isolated concern to you, lieutenant. Like every other man in uniform, from the rawest private to the supreme commander, your prime duty is to serve the cause of victory. Below that is a list of priorities which it is essential you deal with in the correct order. At the bottom of that list is the indulging of personal whims.'

As the column advanced at walking pace along the road, Hood gradually raised his voice so that his words could be heard above the increasing din of battles which were being waged to the left and right as well as directly ahead. But he never shouted loud enough for what he was saying to carry to the men riding behind Steele and himself.

'I'll try to bear all that in mind, captain,' Steele said, and thought he succeeded in concealing how he felt about Hood's response to the brutal incident at Rich Mountain.

The senior officer remained grim faced for a stretched second. Then grinned. 'All that is text book stuff, Mr Steele. But I have it on good authority that it works in practice. You didn't give it a fair try at Rich Mountain. So let's both see how it goes here.'

'Both, sir?'

He shot a sidelong glance at Hood and saw the gaunt face show a fleeting expression of horror and terror as the column of unscathed cavalrymen met and past a straggling group of muddied, bleeding, white-faced soldiers – all of them wounded and three of them struggling to carry a corpse with crimson still trickling from a massive hole in his chest.

'Saw my mother die peacefully in bed when I was twenty five years old, lieutenant,' the captain said after he had composed himself. 'From that day to this, I have never seen another dead person.'

Abruptly, the troop reached the position designated in Hood's orders and looked upon a scene of carnage which Steele considered to be tenfold worse than that he had witnessed at Rich Mountain.

'Welcome to Hornet's Nest, folks!' a bearded artillery sergeant yelled bitterly as he turned away from his twelve-pounder cannon after discharging a shot – the shell blasting through smoke-layered air towards an area where Hamburg River Road curved into a depression and went from sight behind a low rise covered with scrub thickets and oaks.

And when the sound of the explosion was reduced to a ringing in the ears of the newcomers, it was possible to hear just why the area had been given the nickname. For there was

115

a constant barrage of gunfire exchanged between the Union forces behind the rise and the Rebels who waited for an opportunity to charge – creating a sound that would not be unlike that made by a massive swarm of hornets stirred into enraged flight.

'Prepare to attack, captain!' a major with a crimson face roared between the crashing of two cannon shots.

The men were not prepared. Less than half the troopers had seen action before and those who had engaged the enemy had witnessed nothing on this scale.

Under a brightening sky, it could be seen that the Yankees had excellent natural cover on and behind the rise: and that their position was further strengthened by the artillery batteries set up in the open fields which separated the hill from the stalled Rebel advance. Some of the batteries were inactive now, the men who had fired the cannons sprawled on the blood-stained ground beside their guns. But the cost of silencing these guns had been tragically high in Rebel losses.

For the fields were littered with unmoving, grey-uniformed figures who, racing under the arcing shells, had been cut down by murderous fire from the Yankees on the hill. Interspersed among the whole bodies were dismembered limbs, heads and unrecognisable chunks of human flesh – the gruesome remains of men torn apart by exploding shells aimed along a low trajectory into the mass of attackers.

Perhaps the most horrific sight of all was off to one side where, unconcerned by the battle raging a few hundred yards away, a large mongrel dog was tearing the bleeding flesh from a human leg.

'The animal's not hurting anybody, lieutenant!' Hood snapped, just before a bugle-boy sounded the advance. And the world was suddenly filled with a continuous sound of blasting cannons.

Two cavalry troops and more than five hundred infantry-men responded to the signal – plunging out from behind their own artillery to race towards the Union batteries.

The mounted men were on the flanks, carbines firing, many of them shrieking their hatred for the enemy. While between them came the infantry, holding fire.

About fifty yards of ground was gained before there was a lull in the covering fire, while the cannons were reloaded and the mounted men fumbled fresh rounds into their carbines. Which gave the Union troops the opportunity to hit back.

The troopers to either side of Steele tumbled from their saddles without time to vent a vocal response to the bullets plunging into their flesh.

'Sonofabitch!' a man roared and Steele saw Sergeant Perry in mid-air, leaping from his saddle as his horse rolled over, blood spouting from a chest wound.

Smoke billowed and bullets cracked through the acrid-smelling vapour. Screams of pain and terror were now mixed with the war-cries. Horses snorted as they were heeled to faster speeds, heading into the hail of deadly fire directed at the attackers.

'We're gettin' slaughtered!'

'You killed my buddy, you bastards!'

'You crud, you crud, you crud!'

'I'll see you all in hell!'

Racing directly ahead, the men on the ground came together with the riders who had swung in from the flanks – with the intention of gaining a forward position at the centre of the open ground where a battery of four Union fieldguns had been established.

Steele heard the shrieked curses and threats amid the crash of cannon and crackle of small arms. And felt the urge to give voice to his own similar hatred for the enemy. But he checked the impulse and found it remarkably easy to do. And felt a strangely cold anger filling his belly as he let the carbine drop to the extent of its strap, drew the Navy Colt from his holster and squeezed the trigger. Next felt a mirthless grin take command of his features as he saw a Union artillery man stagger backwards and sprawl across a heap of shells – blood oozing from a hole in his chest, left of centre.

It's as easy as killing a rabbit, he thought to himself as he complied with a hand signal from Hood and reined his horse to a halt. Saw that the intended objective had been achieved and snapped his head one way then the other – checking not just on Hood's troop but on the state of the attackers as a whole. And discovered that he was oddly numb to the sight of fresh carnage on all sides of him. Even though the battlefield was made more terrible than before because now the wounded were still in evidence and could be seen and heard as they writhed and screamed in a hundred brands of agony.

117

'Holy Mother of God!' Hood croaked, as Steele steered his horse alongside that of the captain. 'I never thought it would be – '

A half-inch diameter Minie ball entered his back above the left shoulder-blade, mushrooming after impact: and its downward trajectory from the top of the Union-held rise sent the deformed chunk of lead tearing into his heart.

He fell forward, hit the neck of his mount and toppled from the saddle.

Watching the man die, Steele recalled the equally violent death of Sergeant Jacobs. Another regular soldier who had passed on advice to a civilian in uniform before he met his end. This time, Steele could not see which individual among the enemy had done the killing. But he felt no regret about this and was content with such ignorance. Satisfied, too, that he could view the death of Captain Joel Hood so coldly. For it meant the man had not died in vain – at least in terms of another man inheriting some of his wisdom.

Nor, perhaps, in respect of the Confederate cause – although that was something the historians of war would argue about for centuries to come.

A bugle sounded the recall and Adam Steele experienced again the white hot anger which he had mistakenly thought he had conquered.

The Rebel cannons were laying down another barrage and the infantry and the second cavalry troop were racing to withdraw under the artillery cover. While Hood's troop – now under command of Steele – waited for an order to leave the battlefield.

'But – ' he started to blurt to a scared-looking young trooper who gazed at him pleadingly. And bit back on what he intended to say – that the attack had succeeded in gaining the intended ground. And that it was the height of stupidity to withdraw now – an insult to those men who had died in achieving the success. But then he looked away from the trooper and down at the face of the dead Hood.

The captain had no more decisions to make. And right at this moment, Adam Steele was not being asked to make one. Brigadier Anderson had made it. Or Major-General Bragg. Maybe even General Albert Sidney Johnston himself had sent the order down through the chain of command. Whichever, the hounds were being recalled and in the army order of

118

things, Lieutenant Adam Steele had no more right to question the command than the scared-looking young trooper.

'You men heard!' he yelled, as his anger altered from hot to ice cold. 'Get the hell out of here!'

And he was hard on the heels of the troopers, after pausing just a moment to touch the brim of his hat towards the unseeing Hood.

The struggle for the sunken road dubbed the Hornet's Nest raged without let-up from nine-thirty in the morning until four-thirty in the afternoon and there were no further truces for the wounded to be brought behind the lines.

Steele's troop was involved in five of the assaults, losing half its number dead or wounded, before a final mass attack by both divisions of Bragg's Second Corps overran the Union defenders. Which seemed to leave the way open for the Army of the Mississippi to strike a death blow at the forces commanded by Grant.

But it was not to be.

At nightfall, the battle was halted: at a time when the Confederates were poised to gain victory, having driven the enemy back to the banks of the Tennessee River. But General Johnston was wastefully dead, having lost too much arterial blood from a leg wound which would have been relatively minor had it been treated earlier. And his second-in-command, General Beauregard – the hero of the Fort Sumter triumph – neglected to take advantage of Southern gains.

During the evening and night, while Union gunboats fired a constant barrage at the resting Rebels, massive Union reinforcements marched into the Shiloh area. And on Monday morning Grant's army mounted an offensive that pushed the Confederates back off the ground they had so dearly won the day before. At two-thirty in the afternoon, the Rebels left the battleground and, because the Yankees gave no more than token pursuit for a few miles, it was termed a withdrawal rather than a retreat.

Adam Steele was not concerned with what it was called. He now considered he had seen, heard and experienced enough to regard himself as a professional soldier. He had done what was asked of him and had not questioned his orders – at least, had not voiced such questions. And he had not considered his personal feelings in the heat of battle after that moment of hesitation when the bugler sounded recall and he glanced from the trooper to the dead face of Joel Hood.

Now, as he led the depleted column of troopers back towards Corinth, he had the time and the inclination to examine how he felt. And he decided he was satisfied. Not with the result of Bloody Shiloh. Merely that he had survived its slaughter.

'I reckon we got beat, Mr Steele,' Sergeant Perry said grimly from where he rode his horse beside the lieutenant's – the non-com suffering no more than a sprained wrist from having his mount shot from under him at the Hornet's Nest. 'If we had kept on after the bastards Sunday night, we could have – '

'Ours not to reason why, Sergeant,' Steele put in evenly.

Perry spat on to the trail on the other side of his horse from where the officer rode. 'Ours but to do and die. The captain was a good man. And a lot of other good men died for frig all!'

'You bucking for general, feller?' Steele asked.

'No, sir.'

'So leave the top brass to do what they think is right, sergeant. You kill any Yankees in the battle?'

'Six I know of for sure.'

Steele nodded and grinned. 'Then you did right.'

'Guess so, sir.'

Perhaps a half-minute later, as the town of Corinth came in sight, Steele growled softly: 'Happen to agree with you, sergeant.' He scowled. 'Back at Shiloh, we got done.' Now he showed the grimacing non-com another grin. 'But look on the bright side. We didn't get dead.'

THE END OF STEELE'S WAR PART ONE

THE WOMAN: Part Two

'YOU'RE very quiet, Adam Steele,' Lucy Girard said.

'I've got nothing to say,' he answered.

'But plenty to think about, it would seem.'

The war. Why had his mind suddenly filled with vivid memories of the long-ago War Between the States? The recollections had begun with that night in the barn when he proposed marriage to Diana. Now he turned his head to look up at Lucy Girard who sat in the saddle astride the gelding he was leading by the reins.

This full-grown woman of experience looked not at all like the naïve girl Diana Summers had been in those days before the outbreak of war.

But that had just been the starting point for ancient memories. So Edge then? His partnership with the man called Edge during which they had almost always called each other Yank and Reb. In a good-humoured way, though: their attitude towards one another vastly removed from the violent hatreds which had existed between the opposing forces back in the early 'sixties.

Not that it mattered. A man alone did not have to have a clearly defined reason for recalling memories. But right now he was not alone – had had the company of the cruelly cheated mail-order bride for several hours on the slow trek across the floor of the San Simon valley towards the low rises which were called the Peloncillo Mountains on the Arizona-New Mexico border.

'Excuse me,' he said.

'I resent being referred to as a bag, sir,' the red-haired woman countered.

'I did that?'

'Back at the stage stop. You surely recall complaining that you considered yourself hindered by a bag and her baggage?'

'A lady and her valise,' the Virginian said, surveying the terrain on all sides and not looking directly at Lucy Girard. Wondering if he had instinctively maintained his usual vigilance over his surroundings while his mind was concerned with the distant past. 'Excuse me again, ma'am.'

'Who is a burden to you.'

'It's the horse that's carrying you.'

She vented an unladylike snort and hissed: 'You, too, can be a beast at times, sir!'

Another long silence was begun and remained unbroken until, at dusk in the mountain foothills, Steele found a suitable hollow in which to make camp.

'If you tell me what to do, sir,' the woman said evenly, 'I'll be happy to assist with what is necessary. I'm city born and raised.'

Steele helped her down off the gelding. 'You snap twigs off brush for kindling, heap it into a pile, light it and toss on some heavier wood, ma'am. It's called a fire.'

'You hard-bitten sonofabitch!' she rasped, swinging violently away from him and striding to where a thicket of brush grew in the sparse soil on a slope.

As Steele unsaddled the gelding he could hear Lucy Girard muttering angrily to herself while she tore at the brush. Then, as he hobbled the animal, she began to cry softly – perhaps took longer than she needed to build the fire so that she had time to compose herself.

'I don't have a match.'

He dropped down on to his haunches beside the heap of brushwood and set light to it as Lucy stepped back from it. When he rose to stand beside her he saw that she was trembling – trying to stem the motion with her arms akimbo, hands clutched tightly to her shoulders.

'Sit down, ma'am,' he told her. 'Warm yourself. I'll make some coffee.'

'I'm not cold.' In the firelight her eyes were red-rimmed from crying and glistened with fresh tears that threatened to spill down her dust-streaked cheeks.

'But I am, uh?' he said as he moved away to bring the gear from the horse over to the side of the fire.

'I deserve the treatment you have been giving me, sir,' she

replied softly and lowered herself down on to the saddle he set on the ground behind her. Still gripping her shoulders, she added contritely: 'And I'm surely sorry I cursed you like that.'

'Been called worse when I deserved better,' he assured her as he set a coffee-pot to heating in the fire.

'I'm every kind of a stupid fool,' she said tautly. 'Doing what I did and causing so much trouble for people.'

'Isn't anything easier in the world to make than a mistake, ma'am.'

'I've made more than my fair share.'

'Reckon I've been wrong more times than I've been right.'

'Is that what you were thinking about most of the afternoon? The mistake you made in taking a part in the trouble back at that terrible place?'

'No, ma'am. Was maybe trying to decide if I made the right or wrong choice a long time before today.'

'And did you? Come to a decision, I mean?'

'No. And it doesn't matter, anyway. There's no way to undo what was done in the past.'

She sighed deeply. 'That surely is the truth.'

Steele carried just the one tin cup and he offered it to her first after he filled it with strong, hot coffee. She accepted it but then gave it back after taking a sip. Then they traded it back and forth while they ate a spartan meal of cold beans straight from the can and strips of jerked beef.

'We're bound to reach a town of some sort soon, aren't we?' she asked suddenly.

He nodded. 'Not necessarily a town first. But somewhere I can get fresh supplies.'

'On a stage route, perhaps? I don't wish to trouble you longer than is necessary.'

The threat of more tears had gone now and although Lucy was still in the grip of depression there was no sign that she was angling for sympathy from the impassive Virginian seated on the ground beside her. She shivered, then added: 'A different route to the one back there, though. I don't ever in my life want to –'

'We'll see, ma'am. Tomorrow.' He got to his feet, then stooped to unfurl the bedroll. 'Get some sleep.'

'I'm filthy dirty and need to clean my teeth.'

'You and me both. But we don't have the water to spare.'

'Of course,' she said, raising a hand to her mouth. Then added after she stopped chewing on the fleshy side of her thumb: 'I've taken enough from you, Mr Steele. You make use of your own bedding.'

'Get under the blankets, ma'am,' he instructed softly. 'The fire and this will keep me warm enough.'

He held up the sheepskin coat he had separated from the bedroll.

She sighed as she moved from the saddle. 'All right. But only because you told me to.'

Later, after Steele had fixed the fire so that the fuel glowed without causing flames to leap and then stretched out with the saddle under his head, the coat draping his body and his hat over his face, the woman said:

'Why don't you call me Lucy and I call you Adam?'

'Fine.'

'I want to thank you, Adam.'

'Seem to recall you already did.'

'Yes. No, I mean for not getting angry with me when I said about washing and brushing my teeth. I just was not thinking.'

'Sometimes it's better not to, ma'am.'

'Lucy,' she insisted.

'Lucy,' he echoed.

Later still:

'I'm thinking now, Adam.'

Steele sighed into the pitch darkness of his hat. 'Fine.'

'About how different things would have been if it were you and not that terrible Lorrimer man who –'

'Best you go to sleep, Lucy,' the Virginian interrupted. 'That sounds like the stuff dreams are made of.'

Or did it? A mail-order bride and memories of the rainy night and morning with Diana Summers when he asked the girl to marry him. Obviously one woman had triggered memories of the other. And, he realised, his earlier sourness towards Lucy Girard had been an instinctive defence mechanism to keep himself from giving serious consideration to the connection.

Instinctive because of the many long years on long trails when he had been a loner and a drifter – learning in a hard and violent way that his ruling fate had decreed he should never again experience the warmth and security of a deep relationship with a fellow human being. It had taken more

124

than one lesson to teach him to accept his destiny – painfully learned by him and often tragic for those who sought to be more than a mere passing stranger in his harsh life.

But of late, he realised as he peered – weary but not tired – into the darkness of the underside of his hat, there had obviously been a subconscious yearning to reach out and grasp, rather than simply touch, another person.

Renita, the Mexican girl in San Francisco who had turned out to be a whore. The young Sara Yancy up in Oregon. Anne Tucker who he thrust from girlhood into womanhood in a New Mexico town called Nowhere. Gemma Sellers and Lydia Karlsen up in the northern territories. Some of their offers taken, others rejected.

Before them there had been other women: but few and far between in the period when he had resigned himself to his fate. Yet lately, without him being aware of it, one part of his subconscious was apparently demanding that he attempt again to become like other men. While, in another dark recess of his troubled mind, an instinct warned him against it.

But Lucy Girard? Why her?

Because she happened to be convenient. And as willing as she was available. Just as Lydia Karlsen had been, up near Ogallala. In that way, sure. But there had never been any future, even fleetingly considered, in that relationship. As there was with Anne Tucker . . .

The Virginian drifted into sleep. And was not disturbed until he sensed somebody close to him. But felt no compulsion to tighten his grip around the frame of the Colt Hartford that lay beside him under the coat. As he slid the hat off his face and saw the woman standing over him, her body silhouetted against the brightening sky above the eastern mountain ridges.

'Good morning, Adam,' she greeted, turning her head to smile down at him. As she stretched her arms above her head and by accident or design emphasised the generous curves of her body. 'Coffee pot is on and the sun is rising.'

'That's not all that's coming up,' he said huskily. He folded his back away from the ground.

Her smile faded and she swallowed hard as her arms fell down to her sides. 'You mean you . . . ?'

'I mean the coffee can wait.'

She eased slowly down on to her haunches and he could see

125

the pulse at the side of her neck working frantically. 'There's something you should know, Adam,' she whispered. 'I'm not ... there's been another ...'

Steele began to unbutton his shirt, narrowing his eyes as the first warm rays of the new day's sun shafted from between two mountain peaks. His lips drew back to show a smile.

'Just because my name's Adam, I don't have to be the first man.'

'Why, Adam? Why did you change your mind about ...'

He broadened the smile. 'Let's just say that if I decide to marry you, I'd like to know what I'm getting into.'

'Marry me!' she shrieked in shock that hovered on the brink of joy.

He nodded and because his lids were almost cracked closed, she was unable to see the doubt in his coal-black eyes. 'Could be,' he answered evenly, 'that at being single I'm ...

,..ALL THROUGH.' *

*This story is, but Adam Steele's relationship with Lucy Girard (and his memories of the war) will continue in the next book of the series.

The George G. Gilman
Appreciation Society

PLEASE NOTE that
THE GEORGE G. GILMAN
APPRECIATION SOCIETY
will now be operating from
Mr MICHAEL STOTTER,
42 Halstead Road, London, E.11. 2AZ.

NEL BESTSELLERS

T045 528	THE STAND	*Stephen King*	£1.75
T046 133	HOW GREEN WAS MY VALLEY	*Richard Llewellyn*	£1.00
T039 560	I BOUGHT A MOUNTAIN	*Thomas Firbank*	95p
T033 988	IN THE TEETH OF THE EVIDENCE	*Dorothy L. Sayers*	90p
T038 149	THE CARPETBAGGERS	*Harold Robbins*	£1.50
T041 719	HOW TO LIVE WITH A NEUROTIC DOG	*Stephen Baker*	75p
T040 925	THE PRIZE	*Irving Wallace*	£1.65
T034 755	THE CITADEL	*A.J. Cronin*	£1.10
T042 189	STRANGER IN A STRANGE LAND	*Robert Heinlein*	£1.25
T037 053	79 PARK AVENUE	*Harold Robbins*	£1.25
T042 308	DUNE	*Frank Herbert*	£1.50
T045 137	THE MOON IS A HARSH MISTRESS	*Robert Heinlein*	£1.25
T040 933	THE SEVEN MINUTES	*Irving Wallace*	£1.50
T038 130	THE INHERITORS	*Harold Robbins*	£1.25
T035 689	RICH MAN, POOR MAN	*Irwin Shaw*	£1.50
T043 991	EDGE 34: A RIDE IN THE SUN	*George G. Gilman*	75p
T037 541	DEVIL'S GUARD	*Robert Elford*	£1.25
T042 774	THE RATS	*James Herbert*	80p
T042 340	CARRIE	*Stephen King*	80p
T042 782	THE FOG	*James Herbert*	90p
T033 740	THE MIXED BLESSING	*Helen Van Slyke*	£1.25
T038 629	THIN AIR	*Simpson & Burger*	95p
T038 602	THE APOCALYPSE	*Jeffrey Konvitz*	95p
T046 850	WEB OF EVERYWHERE	*John Brunner*	85p

NEL P.O. BOX 11, FALMOUTH TR10 9EN, CORNWALL

Postage charge:
U.K. Customers. Please allow 30p for the first book plus 15p per copy for
each additional book ordered to a maximum charge of £1.29 to cover the
cost of postage and packing, in addition to cover price.

B.F.P.O. & Eire. Please allow 30p for the first book plus 15p per copy for
the next 8 books, thereafter 6p per book, in addition to cover price.

Overseas Customers. Please allow 50p for the first book plus 15p per copy
for each additional book, in addition to cover price.

Please send cheque or postal order (no currency).

Name...

Address...

....

Title..

While every effort is made to keep prices steady, it is sometimes necessary
to increase prices at short notice. New English Library reserve the right to
show on covers and charge new retail prices which may differ from those
advertised in the text or elsewhere. (3)